I0782078

VAMPIRE HUNTER SOCIETY

The Dark Bite

Leia Stone

To Jaymin Eve, the best bestie I could have ever hoped for.

I took one look over my shoulder, making sure that I wasn't followed, and slipped down the alley between 3rd Street and Grant. Tonight's mark had been a challenge to hunt and I was going to be sore as hell tomorrow. My fingers clenched the heavy burlap sack as I stepped up to the nondescript brown, rusted door. I banged three times fast, then once slow, followed by two times fast. A thin eye slit opened, but it was too dark to tell who was on duty. Probably Finn.

"Password." Finn's gritty Irish voice came through the door in a muffled timbre.

"*Daemonium interfectorem*," I whispered.

The metal panel to the right of the door popped open and slid to the left, revealing the hidden keypad underneath. Pressing my finger to the pad, I waited for the soft click of the door mechanism opening. My fingernails still had blood in them from the kill, and my lower back throbbed from being slammed against the wall so hard.

The door clicked and I took one more look down the alley to make sure no one was there, before slipping inside.

Finneas Blight was sitting in his chair, crossbow slung over his back, with dual guns at his sides. As head of security, Finn didn't mess around. His legs were propped up on the worn mahogany desk. Behind him, the House of Rose crest hung on the wall, perfectly lit by the two sconces on each side. Out of the four supernatural hunter houses, House of Thorns, House of Ashes, House of Skulls, and of course House of Rose, we killed the most vampires per year than any other. The other houses took out any supernaturals, but we strictly specialized in the bloodsucking variety.

"Aspen. Did ya get yer mark?" Finn's Irish accent was thick. Normally I didn't dig redheads, but Finn was hot, from his tall muscular physique right down to the reddish-brown, bushy beard. He had a man bun that always rested at the nape of his neck, and at thirty years old had that sexy older guy vibe going on. I'd had a minor crush on him when I was sixteen, but he was nearly ten years older than me. I got over it, and he was happily married now.

I held up the sack, a few drops of blood staining the bottom, and he grinned. "What's that now, sixty?"

I winked. "Something like that."

It was actually seventy-three, the most kills for any junior hunter in the society ever, but I was working on being humble, so I kept that to myself.

Finn waved me forward. "Maz is in back, she'll be happy to hear it."

I slipped through the dingy entryway and into the *real* entrance of our secret society. Two gigantic marble doors pulled back to reveal an opulent foyer: rich hardwood floors, tasteful cream wallpaper, and timeless mahogany furniture.

Kenzley, the butler, greeted me with a grin. "Aspen, lovely to see you. Shall I whip you up something to eat? You must be famished after your hunt."

You never turned down food by Kenz and his staff. He was an incredible chef. "Yes please, but just something quick." I wanted to shower off. Tonight's mark had been hard and I was battle weary, but first I needed to see Maz.

Kenzley disappeared into the kitchen as I traversed the well-lit halls. I passed the library, nodding in greeting to a few of my fellow hunters, raising the bag to show them my kill. Then I moved on to the dormitory, where our hunter apartments all spanned out. The exterior of this building fronted as a nondescript factory, but inside it boasted ten floors, fifty apartments, a large dining hall, youth dormitory, training gym, library, and much more. The Vampire Hunter Society was Spokane, Washington's best kept secret. We took care of the vampire infestation on the entire inland northwest so that the humans never had to know there was even a problem. Eastern Washington, Northern Idaho, and even parts of Montana were well within my hunting territory.

When I reached the two ornately carved wooden doors to Maz's office, I straightened my shoulders, brushing my candy apple red hair out of my face before I knocked.

"Enter!" Maz's singsong voice called out.

I pushed the doors open and she looked up from her desk. "Aspen! Tell me you got him?"

I held up the sack and she thrust her fist in the

air, the sleeves of her priestess robe peeling back to showcase toned forearms. Mazzienne Rose was a sixty-five-year-old badass vampire hunter, woman of God, and the leader of the Spokane branch of our society. I'd looked up to her my entire life, and seeing the approval on her face now made pride swell in my chest.

She pulled out her iPad, brushing a silver lock away from her face, and opened up the photo app. "Let me ID him."

I set the bag down and opened it, peeling the edges back to reveal the head of the dirtbag vampire I'd pulled off of an innocent human.

"He'd been about to drain her," I told Maz, thinking back to the way he'd fed on her, sucking at her neck as she…

I shivered, remembering the human's moan of pleasure.

Disgusting.

Maz glowered. "That's him. Got more complaints about this one than any other. You did good. God bless you, dear." She snapped a photo of the head and then indicated to the incinerator that sat in the corner of her office.

As she typed into her iPad, telling the client we'd taken care of the assailant no doubt, I walked over to the incinerator. Putting on the silicone glove, I peeled open the hatch, a waft of heat lashing out at me as I chucked the head into the fire, before closing the hatch once more. The flames flared to life, consuming the demon completely. I used to be affected by seeing them like this, because they looked *so* human, but then I saw them fight, I saw them kill, I saw what they really were. *Monsters.*

"That's number seventy-three for you. Keep this up and I'm going to have to promote you to senior hunter soon."

I froze. Senior hunter. At nineteen? You didn't get senior hunter until at least twenty-three. My bestie Liv would flip when I told her later.

I finally found my voice. "I would be honored."

Maz nodded, looking up at me with bright blue eyes which were nestled behind a bed of wrinkles. "The bounty has been wired to your account." She tapped something on her iPad.

Only about one percent of the human population knew about or believed in vampires, and the ones who did paid us good money to avenge their fallen or assaulted loved ones. It was our job to protect the humans from the bloodsuckers, and I would step in any day to protect a human free of charge. But the money we made from hired hits helped us keep the organization going for generations. Most of the other hunters within the society were put on patrol at bars and nightclubs that we knew the bloodsucking demons frequented. They kept the humans safe from random vampire attacks.

Some of the bloodsuckers fled Magic City and tried to make a life out here in the human world; others had been here years but get sloppy and we catch them. We were well within our rights to wipe them from the face of the Earth the second they crossed the line from their secret little compound in Northern Idaho. But for me, Liv, Vasquez, and some of the other elite junior and senior hunters, we got the paid gigs, the marks who had done something horrible and needed justice to be served, and God willing, I wanted to be the one to bring those families closure.

My phone buzzed with the incoming wire. Five grand.

Score.

"Thanks, Maz." I headed for the door, tired, hungry, and sore all over.

Her iPad dinged as I was walking out. "Oh, Aspen? How tired are you?"

I spun, wearing a smirk. She always had a mark

for me. Sometimes they took a few weeks to track down, but she always had more.

"I have this other mark…" She fiddled with her pen. "I've sent some of the newer hunters just to tail him, but I just got word that he's at Bang, planning to drain some pretty little blond no doubt. I'd like to take him out now, before he can hurt anyone or gets too comfortable and sets up residence here."

Bang was a nightclub where a lot of unknowing humans went to die. It was a notorious underground feeder club. The lower level was for "VIP" customers, AKA vampires, and if he was there, he was up to no good.

I didn't answer right away. I was tired and she took that as a no. "No worries, I'll send Vasquez."

Freaking douchebag Vasquez? No way.

"No, I can do it." I perked up. "What's the bounty?"

I was tired, but nothing a double shot of espresso couldn't cure. Still, I wasn't going back out hunting for less than five grand.

"This is a *big* mark, Aspen. Your highest profile client yet. He's very dangerous. He just broke out of Magic City Prison." She looked at me with one raised eyebrow.

My tongue instantly stuck to the roof of my

mouth. Magic City Prison? *Holy crap, he must be a big baddie.* Bringing down big baddies brought me untold joy.

Magic City was segregated into six territories, housing all of the supernaturals: vampires, werewolves, witches, light fey, dark fey, and trolls. Magic City Prison was their way of trying to contain their miscreants. If he'd broken out of prison and then escaped the enclave, and was in Spokane, I wouldn't be able to sleep without his head in that incinerator.

"It pays fifty grand," she added.

Fifty grand!

I whistled low. I loved my job, and the society, but I already had a retirement plan in place. Get to one thousand kills and five million bucks in savings, then quit and go buy a private island where I could live on the beach with Liv and whatever hotties we were married to by then.

"There's been chatter of an issue in Vampire City and he's fled to seek refuge here," she said. If there was an issue in Vampire City, that meant the bloodsuckers would flee to the human world and there would be more deaths here—in *my* city. I couldn't have that.

"Send me the details. I'll do it," I told her instantly.

She nodded, but then looked up at me with an unreadable expression. Maz was hard to read sometimes. As a priestess of our secret order, she was basically a nun. She'd devoted her entire life to God and our calling of ridding the Earth of the foul demons called vampires.

"Aspen… there is something you should know about this mark."

I steeled myself, waiting for her to tell me he was a part of the royal family or something.

"He's a Drake. Luka Drake," she finally said, and I nearly choked on my own spit.

He *was* a part of the royal family. "A Drake?"

Maz inclined her head. "Yes. He's the nephew of the queen. But the family paying the bounty is high society. He drained their daughter of blood over ten years ago after asking her on a date. They want closure."

That sick bastard.

"I'll do it. I'll take Liv with me. Split it." If this guy was a member of the Drake family line, I'd need all the help I could get.

She nodded, looking pleased. "Smart. It might take both of you to bring him down."

The mention of the vampire royal family had me nervous. They were powerful, strong, and freaking scary. They also raped and murdered women like it was a hobby. One of our most valuable vampire hunter society members was the Spokane City chief of police. Chief Baker helped make the kill list and passed it down to Maz. He saw the human bodies, drained of blood, prick marks on their neck, positive rape kits. He saw all the ugly and tipped us to who the demon perps were. If this douchebag had killed some innocent chick, then I was bringing his head back. *Tonight.*

After I left Maz's office, I grabbed my food from Kenzley—a yummy breakfast burrito with extra sausage—then took the elevator to my shared apartment with Liv.

She was off tonight, but she'd never pass up twenty-five grand and a chance to bring down Drake royalty. As a part of our training we'd seen pictures of and memorized the entire royal family line ... and that was saying a lot considering there were over a hundred of them. They bred like freaking rabbits.

Using my key, I entered our apartment and grinned when I saw my bestie on the couch, surrounded by popcorn, brownies, ice cream, and candy. She was watching some romantic comedy on TV and crying. Liv was three-days post breakup with douchebag Vasquez, and clearly not handling it as well as I thought.

"Hey, how are you?" I approached the couch with caution. One ice cream container was already empty and on the floor, and I was regretting my decision to take her with me tonight. Maybe she wasn't ready to go back to hunting yet.

She looked up at me and wiped at her eyes. "I'm good. I've decided to become a lesbian."

I forced myself not to smile, and instead pretended to take her seriously. "Okay." I'd known Liv since she was a day old; we grew up in the order's orphanage together. She was straighter than an arrow.

She paused the movie and sat up, looking feral. Her black hair was kinky and unbrushed, flying about her head like a lion's mane. She glared at me with her honey hazel eyes. "Because women aren't cheating, lying, dirtbags who think with their dicks!" she roared.

Ouch. She was definitely in the anger phase of grieving.

"True," I agreed, shoving the last bite of my burrito down my throat. I'd need to shower and change into something super slutty if I was going to Bang and posing as a feeder.

"If Vasquez—" she said his name like it was poison "—wants to screw half the hunters here, then so be it! I'll screw the other half! Including the women. Take *that!*"

This was worse than I thought. Liv and I were both virgins, as outlined in the strict moral code of conduct for female hunters that we adhered to, so I didn't think she was going to go and bang half the hunter squad anytime soon. "You wanna go hunting?" I hedged, "Take out your rage on a member of the vampire royalty?" I tried to switch gears and bring her out of this depression.

Pure joy spread across her face and she grinned, showcasing the dimple in her left cheek. "Yes!"

Liv was passionate, and turning that passion into rage would help tonight. "Get dressed. We're going into Bang as feeders."

"Think there's time to slash Vasquez's tires on the way out?" She raised an eyebrow.

Damn, he really screwed her over. I'd have to have a little talk with him later.

"Maybe later," I lied.

And with that we got ready for one of the most high profile kills of my career. If I brought back the head of a Drake, Maz would surely make me a senior hunter.

usic poured out onto the street as I parked my baby yellow 1967 VW Beetle right in front of Bang. I preferred to hunt a mark in the middle of the day while they slept in their home, but sometimes you didn't have that luxury. The royal family had multiple secret hideouts and offices, much like our society, and tagging one of them usually meant the kill needed to be in public. Public kills meant you couldn't take as many weapons. Liv and I had only packed one six-inch, thin hunting stake each, which we'd tucked into our knee-high boots, and one silver razor wire which would take a vampire's head clean off. That was tucked into the side of my barely-there skirt. Because the vampire's body started to disintegrate right after you killed it, the razor wire was coated in a special serum to preserve the head for identification.

As a failsafe, I had stakes built into the heels of my stilettos, I only needed to uncap them.

Luka Drake was going down tonight.

Supernaturals had been around since the dawn of time, and Maz and her family had been tracking vampires and killing them for generations. If a were-wolf or witch or any of the other supernaturals got out of line, it was up to the other hunter houses to take care of them. House of Rose was strictly a vampire hunting house, and I was proud to be a part of it. We were God-ordained to expunge the demons from this earth and protect human life at any cost.

In order for a vampire to pick you as a feeder, you needed to basically be dressed as a prostitute. My plan was to hopefully get picked as Luka Drake's feeder and just kill him in the feeding room, but if that didn't work, I had plan B and C lined up.

My purse had the little waterproof, lined burlap sack we'd use to transport the head to Maz after the kill; it was shoved inside, folded into a tiny ball. This was minimal hunting at its finest, though I still longed for my well-equipped hunter duffle bag with all of its fancy crossbows and metal spikes.

When Liv and I stepped out of my car, every male's head turned in our direction, causing Liv to smile. She loved that kind of attention. I, however, wanted to shrink into a ball and disappear. I didn't like skeezy men staring at my bare legs.

We waited impatiently in the long line, and finally got in after forty-five minutes. I didn't want to tip any suspicions by pulling strings to get on the list. Vampires were very aware of hunters and how well connected we were. Anything like that might blow our cover. Liv and I had just turned nineteen, only two months apart, but we had the best fake ID that money could buy, so tonight we were twenty-two.

Once we made it inside, I was assaulted with loud music and flashing lights. The bass thumped across my chest as a frantic rhythm echoed across the dancefloor and we beelined it for the VIP section. Because of vampires' super sensitive hearing, I had to talk to Liv in code.

"If I find a guy and you can't find me, just meet me at home, okay?"

That meant if shit hit the fan or something went wrong and we were split up, we would meet back at the society.

She nodded and we both glanced at our watches, complete with GPS tracking. I was now synced with her in case we split up. I could find her via the watch.

We stepped up to the VIP bouncer, a tall vampire with white-blond hair who was barely moving. I could not only smell the coppery scent wafting off of him but see what he was by his too-pretty features and pale skin.

Demon.

I sent up a quick prayer to God to help me pretend to be normal in front of this foul abomination, all in an effort to serve the greater good. Like taking down Luka Drake.

I rolled my shoulders back, sticking my boobs out to catch his gaze. "I hear downstairs is more fun. Can we come play?" I purred and bit my bottom lip for effect. I was wearing my long black wig, the fake hair touching my lower back. I was constantly having to change my appearance in order to not be recognized, as hunters were well known within this club.

Liv slapped my butt and I yelped, glaring at her.

The vamp grinned, pulling back the rope to allow us entry into the sordid feeding pit. As we walked past him, he inhaled my scent and it took everything within me not to punch him in the balls and take his head to Maz.

Focus on Luka. Luka is the mark, I had to tell myself.

Sashaying my hips back and forth, I led Liv and I downstairs. The smell of blood was thick in the air and it made my adrenaline spike, as well as my anger. When I'd started my training for the society at twelve years old, I underwent three voluntary genetic modifications. One for enhanced smell, one for enhanced speed, and the final for enhanced strength. I was nowhere near as fast and strong as a vampire, but I could hold my own. We had some of the brightest scientists and doctors in our organization, and a simple gene editing treatment with a few injections before puberty was all it took.

The cocktail waitresses on these lower levels were all vampires. One of them walked over to us now, lips tinged slightly red. "Hello, ladies, can I get you a drink?"

I absentmindedly ordered two drinks for us while my gaze searched the space, mentally flipping through images in my head of the entire Drake royal family. The king was murdered last year by a were-wolf, and the queen rarely left Magic City. The ones who lived here in the human world only left their secretive lair for a night of debauchery, leaving human bodies in their wake.

My mind flew to Morgana Drake, sister to the late king and aunt to my mark Luka. The Drakes had a farm somewhere north of here where they popped out babies in their human form and then changed them to vampires in order to keep their DNA pure and living forever. If I ever learned where the Drake farm was, I'd drop a bomb on it and never look back. Those people were sick.

"Have fun, babe!" Liv called out, gyrating her pelvis as she let a male vampire take her hand and lead her onto the dancefloor.

That was our public code for *Happy Hunting*. If I wanted to find Luka, I needed to mingle.

I grinned. "Have fun."

I'd been hunting with Liv since we were fifteen. Maz adopted us into the society from a local orphanage in Idaho when we were merely babies, so we hunted together well.

Split up and get immersed in the vibe, do whatever it

takes to get close to the mark and then kill him swiftly before escaping with his head.

I'd been so lost in my thoughts, I hadn't noticed the vampire approach me.

"Care to dance?" His smooth buttery voice called in my ear from behind me.

I spun, and my heart skittered in my chest as I came face to face with Luka Drake.

Holy bloodsucker.

I swallowed hard as I let my gaze rake over him slowly. His dark hair was slicked back, showcasing his strong jaw and entrancing eyes, which were buttery yellow right now with black at the edges. A human might think it was a trick of the light, but I knew better. He was *hungry*.

His tight green t-shirt hugged his muscles like a second skin and I couldn't help but gawk at the tattoos covering his neck, arms and the tops of his hands. It seemed his face was the only surface area unmarked by the artwork.

I tried to control my features, letting go of the surprise I felt that my mark had come right to me. Luka was the eldest son of the late Marcus Drake, and if my information was correct, Queen Drake's hated little nephew—felon, black sheep of the family, and devastatingly handsome.

Vampire or not.

Luka flashed me a smile that would melt the panties off any normal girl, but instead my stomach roiled. These demons were sexier than sin, and I had to constantly remind myself that they were blood-sucking monsters, and pray that I didn't fall into their trap of sensual appeal. He'd drain me and leave my body for dead without a second's thought.

Focus.

"Sure let's dance." I grinned, playing the role. My gaze flicked to the dancefloor. Holy crap, Thorin Drake was here. *Three* members of the royal family were here tonight. That meant something big was going on. They never congregated together in public for fear of an attack that could wipe a large number of them out.

Luka gently took my hand and led me to the dancefloor and I eyed my exits. The VIP lounge was in the basement. The only exit was back past the bouncer or through a tiny vent window in the bathroom. I wouldn't be able to kill him here in public and get away with it, but I could if I lured him to a feeder room, or even the bathroom under the premise of a sexual encounter…

We smooshed against dancing bodies until we found an opening and then Luka placed his hands on my hips. "Is this okay?" he asked, leaning in to whisper into my ear as I felt him inhale my scent.

Hah! He was asking consent to touch my hips? That was hilarious considering he'd drained a girl and killed her. What a two-faced douchebag. I didn't trust myself to speak, so I just nodded and pressed myself closer to him, hoping to lure him into a feeding room soon so I didn't have to pretend to like him much longer. I started to dance, raising my hands in the air and thrusting my hips in a circular motion against him, all the while planning my attack once we were alone.

I peered over his shoulder and noticed Liv dancing with Thorin now. As far as I knew, Thorin wasn't on any hit list, but that didn't mean she wasn't allowed to kill him. It just meant she wouldn't be paid for it. Any vampire who wasn't living either in Magic City or in Delphi, a secret campus for banished magical rejects here in Spokane, was fair game.

If Liv and I could kill both Thorin and Luka, that would be unreal. Two less Drakes in the world was a better world to live in.

Luka looked down at me from behind long dark lashes and I couldn't help but remark at how utterly good looking he was. Like… whoa.

"I like these." He trailed a finger up the outer edge of my thigh where my rose tattoos were and my body responded, sending a pool of warmth between my legs.

No. Resist the devil's charms.

Leaning forward, I gave him a sweet smile, and changed the topic. "Are you here with friends?"

He licked his lips, eyeing mine sensually, and nodded. "Family actually."

Okay, maybe this idiot would talk. "Cool! Me too! My sister," I lied and pointed to Liv, who was grinding on Thorin, Luka's three-hundred-year-old uncle who looked twenty-five.

Luka looked at Liv, slight confusion at my sister comment, probably comparing our different skin tones, and nodded. "Would you girls like to come back into the VIP party room? Free food and drinks all night."

Yes! That was the feeding room.

"Sure! I thought this was VIP." I giggled, trying to act like a dumb chick.

He grinned, and holy hell he *was* gorgeous. I inspected his neck covered in tattoos, and the words "Five Crew" were scrawled across his collarbone in black ink, causing me to wonder what it meant. I wouldn't lie, grinding against his hard toned body was having an effect on me I wasn't proud of.

This demon's magic was strong. I was getting distracted.

"It is, but this is a little more exclusive." Luka winked and my stomach involuntarily warmed.

"Cool." I reached out and laced my fingers through his, cold to the touch, and then we walked over to Liv and Thorin. I tapped Liv on the shoulder, waving for her to follow us.

Luka and Thorin shared a look and nodded.

Once we got back there, I'd have to find a private, curtained feeding room and kill him quickly and quietly. Technically, Liv could kill him too, it didn't matter which one of us took him down. But I'd already partnered off with him, so she could take Thorin and we'd both go down in hunter history. Two Drakes in one night!

Luka led me to the far back wall with a black curtain covering the entrance and two huge beefy vamps standing before it. They took one look at their prince and nodded, opening the curtain without a word. I'd never been back here before, but a few other society members had. From what they reported, there were little closed-off curtain rooms for feeding and a private bar to keep the humans nice and inebriated. I'd been fed on just one other time, for a few seconds before I'd managed to kill the bastard, and the weirdest part was that it felt *good*. The vampires injected a small amount of something akin to a mild narcotic into your blood to make you more pliable. It was similar to a Vicodin and it kept you wanting more. I was willing to be fed on again if it meant getting the job done, but I prayed it wouldn't come to that.

We ascended two levels of stairs, which I esti-mated now put us at a secret top floor level, and Thorin pulled Liv off into the direction of a red-curtained room. She and I shared a look that needed no words. We'd kill both of these assholes quickly and meet back at my car for a quick getaway. Luka led me down a hallway and into a main room with a bar in the center, dozens of curtained rooms at the perimeter. Liv must have gone into a different, smaller feeding area...

"Nephew!" a deep, raspy voice called out behind me and I spun.

Dear God, give me strength.

My hand tightened in Luka's involuntarily as I stared at Keres Drake, the mad king. I ... thought he was dead. Keres was unseated from his position as king by Drucilla Drake, the current queen. All because he'd lost his mind. He was over two thousand years old, and at that kind of age, the immortal just craved an end. I stared at the open socket where his left eye used to be and swallowed hard.

Rumor had it that he went so crazy he yanked out his own eye in a fit and then … ate it, all before he killed his own wife and daughter, leading Drucilla to challenge his ability to lead. He was absolutely the most horrifying vampire I'd ever laid eyes on.

Even though he sort of looked about thirty years old, there were cracks in his skin that just weren't natural, like his flesh was diseased. His eyes ran up and down my body in a hungry gaze and he grinned, teeth bloodstained. "What do you have here, dear boy? A homecoming present?"

I involuntarily turned into Luka for protection as he pulled me toward his body, laying a protective hand around my hip.

"Hello, Uncle," Luka ground out, tension thick in his voice. He was clearly not in favor of this vampire.

That was interesting.

"And who are you?" His one eye snapped to me as he wet his lips again and I forced myself not to recoil.

"I'm Amelia." I threw out a fake name, my voice betraying some of the fear I felt.

Keres stuck his hand out, like he expected me to kiss it. Against everything inside of me, I reached out my hand and grasped his fingers lightly, shaking his cold dead hand like I was yanking a dry, brittle, wooden stick.

Keres' nostrils flared, and I thought he was taking in my scent, then alarm registered in his single widened eye.

"The Shadow Bloods," he hissed, and Luka threw me to the ground so quickly I could barely register what was happening.

My chest slammed into the tile floor as I lay flat as a pancake beneath Luka's body, who hovered over me.

Did he say *Shadow Bloods?*

The Shadow Bloods were vampire mercenaries, even more lethal than we were, but they didn't do it for God and country. They were vampires who worked for mafia families that had beef with royalty. If they were here, it meant Thorin, Keres, and Luka were all about to die. They would kill Liv and I too, just for fun. They hated hunters, we were competition. Luka's weight suddenly left me and I growled from my place on the floor. Popping up to my feet, I stood just behind Luka. No way were these bloodsucking thugs taking my mark!

Reaching into my boot, I pulled out my silver stake. I would kill him now and use the Shadow Bloods as a distraction.

Luka was in a fighting stance, eyes pinned on the door, waiting for the Shadow Bloods to burst in any moment. Keres bolted for the exit. I lunged forward, ready to stab this stake right into Luka's back and through his heart. I only needed to weaken him enough to get him to drop to his knees, then I could take his head. The tips of all my weapons, including this stake, were laced with the potion that would preserve a vampire's body for a day so we could take the heads and it would look like a normal murder to human police. Chief Baker took it from there.

I lunged forward, ready to make the kill, when Luka, faster than I'd ever seen a vampire move, blurred before me and caught my arm midair, just as the door behind him blew off its hinges.

"Hunter?" Luka hissed, looking at me wide-eyed, confused and … hurt? Grabbing my lower back with one hand while keeping my stake hand pinned between both of our chests, one jump and we were airborne, flying up into the exposed ductwork ceiling. This portion of the VIP room wasn't in the basement. We'd gone up to the attic, and the ceiling was a good twenty feet high, with exposed rafters and steel beams.

My stomach lurched and I had to fight to keep from screaming. What the hell was he doing? He'd just identified me as a hunter. I was holding a freaking stake! And now he was what, kidnapping me?

He had to make a split-second decision then: drop the one hand holding me to him, or drop the hand keeping me from stabbing him in the chest with my pointy silver stake I tensed, preparing to be dropped right on top of the Shadow Bloods, but he chose the latter. Keeping my body pressed to his, hand firmly around my waist, he released the pressure on my stake hand and used his free arm to snake out and hold on to a metal rafter, pulling us onto a skinny beam. The metal groaned but held, as he used his leg to pull us deeper up onto the beam.

He knew I was a hunter and he didn't drop me? He hadn't killed me yet? Why? I was completely frozen in shock, unsure what to do.

The small beam Luka had rolled us onto was right next to a large duct, and a perfect hiding spot from the Shadow Bloods. He pivoted our bodies so that I was smooshed between him and the metal ducting at my back.

I was essentially trapped underneath his body, my stake arm free to do some stabbing, but I paused. My heart hammered against my chest as his hips pressed into mine to keep him from falling backward. His buttery yellow eyes burned into mine as my chest heaved, pressing my breasts against him. In all the struggle, my black wig slipped halfway off and he stared at my bright red hair which had come loose and spread across my arm.

A male's bloodcurdling scream rang out below then. Was that Thorin?

Liv!

I jerked upright, but Luka's hand came down on my shoulder, slamming me back onto the platform.

He shook his head, warning me not to move. All I could do was breathe and watch the golden flecks in his eyes while I wondered why he'd chosen not to drop me. He could have left me for dead … or killed me himself.

I wouldn't be able to live with myself if I let Liv just be killed by the Shadow Bloods. They would end her life without a second's thought. I craned my neck, having to move closer to Luka in order to do it, and looked down. My throat went dry at the sight of at least six Shadow Blood mercenaries who had entered the feeding room. They had Thorin on his knees, sword at his throat.

I didn't see Liv. I searched frantically until I remembered my watch. Wriggling my arm free, I pulled my watch up, attracting the attention of Luka. Liv's little GPS dot was moving away from the club, and I sagged in relief against him.

Thank God. She got away.

Luka looked at my watch and then at me, eyes slitted as anger—no, rage—played out behind his features, and his gaze flicked from my watch to my wig, to the stake in my hand. Guilt wormed through me for half a second until I remembered I was literally feeling bad for betraying a blood-drinking demon from hell!

I mentally recited my favorite *Hunter Scriptures* verse, the one that kept me fighting the darkness every single day even if I wanted to quit: *"For we, as ambassadors of heaven, fight not our fellow humans, but against the foul demons of this world. Demons who feed on the life blood of humanity."*

"Where is the prince!?" the Shadow Bloods below questioned Thorin.

The vampire stayed silent, and my gaze flicked up to Luka's face. He was … wrestling with something. He wouldn't … give himself up … to save his douchebag uncle, would he? He pulled himself up and over me, trying to get some leverage, his back against the ceiling.

Was he going to jump down? I shimmied under him, leaving the silver stake on my chest, and reached my hands out, latching on to his forearms with an iron, vise-like grip. He looked down at me incredulously and I shook my head.

Don't do it, you idiot.

Six freaking Shadow Bloods would murder us all. They were highly trained vampires with backup plans upon backup plans. His first instinct—to hide—was the right one. Six inside this room meant a dozen outside on the VIP floor. This was a well-planned assault. One I'd gotten myself stuck in the middle of.

"Last time," the man holding the blade to Thorin's throat growled. "Where. Is. Prince Luka?"

Luka strained against my hold and I opened my thighs, wrapping my legs around his waist, and clenched. This bastard was going to get himself killed, and for what? To save a murdering, blood-draining asshole like Thorin? And no doubt give away my hiding spot in the process…?

No way.

Why was I saving this bloodsucker from killing

himself? I had no idea. Maybe it was because he could have killed me by now, or dropped me, and he hadn't. Maybe there was such a thing as a decent vampire. No, I shook my head at that last thought. He probably saved me because he was hungry and knew if he got stuck up here too long, he'd need a snack.

Luka looked down at me again, eyes glowing copper, nostrils flaring as I held on to him with everything I had. We both knew he could shake me off if he really wanted to, but I was trying to buy time for him to think this through. His eyes fell to my lips, then I felt him harden, his erection growing between us. I unclenched my legs and opened my mouth in shock, swallowing my gasp as a halfcocked grin swept across his face. Luka pulled himself away from me a few inches, giving us both some room to breathe.

Was he ... *attracted to me?* The thought was horrifying. I mean I had straddled him, but ... he was a demon.

Hell spawn.

I shook myself, trying to expunge it all from my brain.

Why was I so mortified?

Thorin met his death then, while Luka was busy

bonering out over my little wrestling move. The sound of cutting bone was one I was extremely familiar with. I didn't have to look to know that Thorin's head had just been taken off. The thud to the floor confirmed it.

Luka winced, looking down at me with anger, and … confusion. Either way, I was just glad it was no longer arousal or amusement at my shock of his … display.

"I hear a rapid heartbeat," one of the Shadow Bloods said, and my eyes went wide. "There's a scared little human in here."

Crap. One thing I couldn't change, no matter how much gene editing I'd had. Heartbeat and human smell.

"I don't give a fuck about a human. I want the prince!" another male shouted.

"We were supposed to do this tonight. Morgana won't be pleased," the other said.

Luka's entire body stiffened at the mention of Morgana.

Holy crap! Did his own family order a hit on him? It sure as hell sounded like that. My eyes flicked up to meet his and I saw the moment he realized he was betrayed by his own blood. Complete and utter pain crossed his features before he quickly stowed it away and it was replaced by a cold hard grimace.

A walkie-talkie squawked. "All clear out here. Have you got the target? Over."

The dude sighed. "Negative. Cancel mission. Over and out."

"Fuck!" The one guy kicked the wall, and then shuffling footsteps could be heard.

I presumed they were gone.

Luka lay against me, staring off at the wall as if replaying his family's betrayal over and over in his mind. We stayed like that, pressed together, lost in our own thoughts, for about five minutes, until he pulled himself up and off of me.

"We should go," he ground out, grabbing me by the waist and yanking me to his chest. I tried not to yelp as he casually carried me like I was a five-pound Barbie Doll, and leapt off the rafter. As we dropped to the floor, he released me and set me gently on my feet.

The stake was still in my hand. His uncle's head lay on the floor near the rest of his body, both withered to a black husk, soon to be ash. There was no coming back from decapitation, not even for a vampire.

I looked over at Luka, who seemed beside

himself. More so than I thought he should be. But he did save my life, and I had a moral code that would not allow me to forget that.

"Thank—" I'd been about to thank him when someone lunged out from behind one of the feeding room curtains.

"I knew it!" a Shadow Blood yelled. He had been hiding in there the entire time.

Both Luka and I exploded into action as he reached for his walkie-talkie.

I drove my stake six inches into the arm that reached for the radio before he could even say a word. His scream ripped through the feeder room as he dropped the radio, and Luka went right for his throat, grasping his neck with both hands. A vampire could easily rip another vampire's head off, especially Luka. As a member of the royal family, he had the most potent kind of genes. His power would be unmatched, but the Shadow Bloods were a well-trained mercenary group. I yanked my stake back out and the dude pivoted, throwing himself forward, and wrenched out of Luka's grasp.

Frick.

I pulled my stake back up just as the guy reached me. Lashing out, I aimed to stab him in the chest, but he moved so fast, a blur, that I only grazed his shoulder.

A door slammed somewhere just beyond me and then we were joined by two more Shadow Bloods. Some of the men from before had come back.

Awesome.

This was how I was going to die.

Luka sped across the space and positioned himself so that his back was pressed to mine. "You watch my back and I'll watch yours, okay, hunter?" His voice was deep and throaty and did not at all hold the fear I was feeling right now.

Fighting back to back with a freaking vampire? Did I have any other option right now?

"Fine," I growled, just as the bastards reached us.

The tall one with a shaved head launched at me, but I was ready for him. Keeping my back to Luka, I kicked out, landing a boot squarely in the guy's balls. He crumpled forward and I came down with my stake like a psycho, stabbing wildly into his back, trying to reach his heart. Luka was pushed into me suddenly, which caused me to go forward, nearly losing my balance. I knocked into the vampire that I'd just poked a bunch of holes into, and he stood up quickly, cracking his head into my chin.

Pain exploded in my jaw and I lost balance,

allowing the vampire to grip me by the shoulders. He sneered at me, his fangs distending.

"Hunter," he seethed.

I'd never heard of a Shadow Blood capturing one of us and just letting us go.

Tonight I would probably die—but I wouldn't go out without a fight. I puckered my lips and spat in his face, then reeled my head forward, slamming my forehead into his nose, grinning as the satisfying crunch of breaking bone filled the room.

"Bitch!" he roared and then chucked me across the room, in one clean arc.

This is going to hurt...

I braced myself for the hit, crashing into a table and chairs, which helped to break my fall. My butt slammed into the table first and I skidded backward, taking out a chair on my way to the ground.

Ow. That was going to bruise.

My gaze flicked to Luka to see that he was fighting the other two Shadow Bloods barehanded, no weapons, just repeating blows to the face.

I popped onto my feet, readying myself for the Shadow Blood who had chucked me across the room to come back and finish me off. He ran at me full speed. I braced myself. Reaching into my skirt, I yanked the razor wire free just as the bastard slammed into me, knocking me backward. I tried to steady myself for the hit but he was too powerful and I lost balance. The force at which he plowed into me had my head cracking backward onto the hard floor.

One smack and everything went dark.

I came to and my heart raced as my fight-or-flight instinct kicked back in. Peeling my eyes open, I frowned in confusion. I was no longer on the floor of the feeder room in the club. I was … in a bed. Soft gray silk sheets brushed against my skin as I tried to sit up—and a raging headache slammed into me. I winced as my fingers probed the knotted bruise at the base of my skull.

What the…? Where was I?

I inhaled.

Luka.

This freaking bed smelled of Luka! I should know, I was smooshed under his body for ten minutes in the rafters of the club. A fact that made my stomach warm, something I was not proud of.

Why the heck was I in his bed? What had happened after the Shadow Blood had knocked me out?

Pulling off the bedspread, I gasped when I saw dried blood on my legs and shirt. *A lot* of blood. I quickly lifted my shirt and did a body scan, relieved to find the blood wasn't mine. Swinging my legs over the edge of the bed, I noticed my boots lined up at the far wall. Padding away from the bed, I slipped them on and then opened the bedroom door.

The first thing I noticed was more blood. It started at the door handle, then trailed down the hall, puddling on the hardwood floor.

"Luka?" My heart knocked against my chest.

What if this wasn't Luka's place, what if it was the Shadow Bloods and I was a late-night snack?

I heard a muffled groan, like an injured animal, and started running.

When I turned the corner into the open living room, a startled scream died in my throat.

Luka lay draped across the couch, a giant wound bleeding freely at his abdomen. It was so big I could see his intestines. He was shirtless, covered in tattoos and blood, and I didn't know what to do.

This bloodsucker was everything I hated. I'd built my life around killing his kind, but in that moment I went into damage control.

"Why aren't you healing?" I gasped.

His skin was whiter than white, his eyes void of their normal glossiness. He was circling the drain. Those Shadow Bloods had jacked him up bad, and he must have carried me here, bleeding all over the place.

Idiot. Why would he do that?

"Silver … wound," he rasped, barely able to get the words out.

Crap.

That delayed healing, but he would be okay if he was able to feed.

"I'll call one of your feeders." I looked around for a phone. My purse was gone and I was missing my watch. Royalty had about a dozen feeders at their beck and call, all paid six figures with big, fat, signed NDAs.

He shook his head. "Can't trust … any … one. All … want me … dead."

Morgana. I'd forgotten about that. Did he think one of his feeders would turn on him? Give up his location? I didn't know anything about their relationship, but clearly it was bad. What did this guy do to deserve such hatred from his own aunt?

"I'll go to the hospital. Steal blood." I looked around for some car keys or something. For some reason I just couldn't walk away and leave him to die, not after he carried me here when he could have left me unconscious and allowed the Shadow Bloods to kill me.

I've never not killed my mark.

Never.

Until now.

His hand reached out and grasped mine and I was shocked at how cold his fingers were. More than normal vampire cold.

"Dead blood. Need … fresh," he rasped.

Oh.

Oh. No.

Chills ran up my arms as the realization hit me. I was going to have to let him feed from me if I wanted him to live. Why was I even entertaining this!? This was a douchebag vampire of the royal family! He'd been about to feed on me in that room right before the Shadow Bloods dropped in. So … why didn't I just let him die?

An ache bloomed in my chest at the thought. He

was … different. Not that I'd gotten to know many vampires, but the way he so quickly made the split decision to pull me up into the rafters with him, even after he knew I was a hunter … it changed everything.

His fingers still grasped mine, weakly, but he held on. In his own way he was asking without asking.

Aspen, you are a stupid woman, I told myself as I dropped to my knees.

You hunt these animals, not keep them alive! I raged at myself as I draped my hair across one shoulder, exposing my neck.

You protect humans from being fed on like animals, you do not willingly give your blood.

I leaned forward and pressed my neck to his lips. *You…*

Pleasure exploded inside of me as two sharp pricks sliced into my neck.

This was different from when I'd been fed on before. Although that had felt good, it was also scary and predatory, but this was … *orgasmic.* All of these weird feelings and thoughts flooded my system all at once. Trust, adoration, life, vitality, love, bond, darkness, all of these words and feelings swirled around my head as pleasure pulsed through my body like a wave of heat. Tingly warmth spread between my legs, and I reached up and threaded my fingers through his hair, pushing him harder into my neck. I moaned at the same time he did, and his hand came around my back to trail my spine.

Holy vampire hunter. What was this magic?

Dizziness washed over me then and he pulled back, licking the spot he had bitten with his tongue, sending chills down my spine.

Whatever spell he'd held over me broke in that moment, and cold ice water flushed through my veins as I instantly sobered.

I let a demon feed off me…

God forgive me.

I sat back, hand flying to my neck as I met his gaze in shock.

We were both wearing a look that said, *What the heck was that?* Which told me that wasn't a normal feeding session for him.

His eyes were alight, copper threaded with gold; he looked more alive than ever. I peered down at his abdomen, gasping as the skin knitted together supernaturally, covering the wound.

'That was weird. I felt her emotions,' he said. But his mouth didn't move…

I jumped up, stumbling backward, and tripped over the coffee table, falling on my ass.

What the hell!

His eyes went wide.

'Can you hear me?' His voice… inside my head. No mouth moving.

"No." I put my hand out. "No. No. No. Whatever demon magic this is—NO WAY."

"Oh shit." Luka looked at me differently then, like he was… scared of me, or this, whatever this was.

I needed to get out of here. I'd saved his life and now we were even. I needed to scram and pretend this never happened.

Bolting upright, I ran to the door in long strides. My purse sat on an entryway table along with my busted-up watch. Grabbing everything in my hands, I yanked open the front door.

He called out: "Wait, we have to talk about th—"

I slammed the door behind me and ran.

I was in a stairwell, taking them down two at a time as my thoughts raced a mile a minute. Vampires didn't have mind speaking powers … or as far as I knew they didn't. Maybe because he was royal he did. But why the heck did I have them with him? A whimper left my throat.

My hands shook as I reached the metal EXIT door. Kicking it open, I burst outside and spun, taking stock of my surroundings.

I recognized where I was immediately. This was a

seedy part of town, probably his hidden bolthole his family never knew about. Slipping my purse over my shoulder, I powered up my phone and started to walk in the general direction of the society. We had smaller safe houses for emergencies, but I didn't want to go there. I need to talk to Liv first. She picked up on the first ring.

"Where in the name of all things holy are you? I've been freaking out," she screamed, and I yanked the phone away from my ear to avoid going deaf.

"I'm safe. Come meet me at the ice cream place." Code. "Tell Maz I'll get her proof the job was done."

Without the head, Maz only paid us fifty percent of the bounty, because it could be fake and she'd been scammed by a few hunters in the past who weren't actually killing. In our hunting career, we were allowed three blood evidence cases, and so this would be my first. Ever since then, she put the incinerator in her office and required the head. I just hoped all of this blood on me was actually Luka's.

Liv knew better than to ask any more questions, not after I used our ice cream place code. It was the most severe of codes we had.

WW3. Nuclear. Ride or freaking die.

"On my way," she said, and the line went dead.

I jumped in an Uber going west and pulled out

my phone as the driver looked at me wide-eyed. I'd forgotten I was covered in blood.

"I'm a model. Just got off a crazy zombie shoot," I told the guy gripping the wheel with white knuckles. He relaxed a little after that, but only a little.

Going into my contacts, I pulled up Maz's number and sent her a text.

Me: Things got complicated last night. Will give a full report later. Job is done.

If I didn't report about killing Luka, someone else would go after him, and I didn't know how I felt about that just yet…

I turned my phone off and leaned my head against the cool glass window, my fingers going to the two prick marks at my neck.

Holy hell, Aspen, you have royally screwed up this time.

I PACED the entrance of Riverfront Park, getting stares from people as I realized I must look like a murderer.

"Good lord, Aspen!" Liv's voice came from behind me and I spun. She was holding my bug-out backpack firmly. She took one look at my appearance and winced. "What happened last night?"

I grabbed the bag from her and pulled out my trench coat, throwing it over my bloody clubbing outfit. I slung the bag over my shoulder and we started to walk.

"Prince Luka … saved my life." I hated the words as they left my mouth.

She frowned. "Why would he do that?"

"I dunno. But … then I saved his."

She looked horrified. "Why would *you* do *that*?"

I stopped and faced her, feeling overwhelmed by my own emotions. My entire life I'd spent hating the bloodsuckers, bringing them down as a servant of God, and now … my world felt like it was shifting on its axis. "I don't know, okay. He was a decent dude, he carried me to safety from the bar even with his guts hanging out of his stomach … and he was dying. I felt bad. So … I let him feed from me." I pulled my hair back to reveal my neck and she gasped, hand flying to her throat. "And I think we…" I remembered when he spoke into my mind. "I dunno, it was different. I think we imprinted or some demon magic. Like the wolves do."

My best friend's eyes widened to giant saucers

and she stood there for a full minute staring at me like I'd sprouted two heads.

I reached out and shook her. "Liv … breathe. You're scaring me."

"Surely imprinting is a myth," she finally said, "and even if it's true, it's only for werewolves and *certainly* not humans."

Her confidence made me feel better. "Yeah, that's what I thought." Maybe I'd imagined the mental speaking thing.

She pulled me over to a bench and yanked me down to sit with her. "But … why would you think you imprinted or whatever?"

I took in a deep breath and described the feeding. In detail. Including the intense sexual energy of it and when I'd heard him speak into my mind. She grimaced through the entire thing and I was mortified beyond belief.

"Well … that does sound different, but maybe you were just horny. I mean, you haven't had a boyfriend since Sterling—"

"Liv! Get real," I shouted. "I'm not horny, and that doesn't explain hearing his voice in my head after!" I winced when a passerby glared at us. Shouting *horny* in the middle of a public park wasn't even the low point of the last twenty-four hours, and that was just sad.

Liv nodded, her tight dark curls shaking around her shoulders. "Well, that was just a hallucination fueled by panic."

"Really?" Maybe she was right. Maybe I was freaking out for no reason. I relaxed at her reassurances.

"Close your eyes. Do you hear him now?" she coaxed me.

I did as she said.

Hello?

Nothing. But … I did *feel* different. When I concentrated on the feeling, it was like … I could feel *him*, like I knew how he was doing, what he was feeling. He was … confused, scared.

No. I was imagining that.

My eyes snapped open. "Nope. Don't hear anything."

The best thing I could do now would be to forget the whole thing happened and go on with my life.

"You need to keep your neck covered until that crap heals. Maz would lose her mind." Liv eyed the angry puncture marks on my neck that I stroked with my fingers. One of the DNA modifications I'd underwent did speed up healing, but nothing vampire level. It would still take a day or two for this to disappear completely.

I nodded. "So you don't think I need to go on the run and leave the society?" I clutched my bug-out bag, thinking of the exit plan that Liv and I put in place in case things ever went sideways.

Liv barked out in laughter. "Wouldn't be the first time a hunter has willingly let a vampire feed from them, won't be the last. Come on, let's go home."

Liv and I grew up in the society. We were raised by hunters and Maz, who told us some pretty crazy vampire hunting stories. Liv was right, this wasn't the first time, and her nonchalance was making me feel tons better.

"Yeah, no biggie," I said, but the knot in my stomach told me it was a very big thing indeed.

ONCE WE GOT BACK to the society, I covered my neck with a scarf and gave Maz a modified rundown of everything that had happened.

"Cursed Shadow Bloods!" she rasped as she took a dried blood sample from my shirt to identify Luka Drake's DNA. In place of a head, this was the next best thing. Why was I lying and saying he was killed? Why didn't I just say he got away?

Partly because I'd never not taken a mark—and because then she'd send a bigger team after him and he'd die. He saved my life … twice. I just wasn't ready to kill him yet.

The machine that she'd put the blood sample into beeped.

"Luka Drake. Well done," she said, and my phone buzzed. She'd paid me the twenty-five grand. I almost sagged in relief.

"I have something else I want to speak with you about," she said, and panic flared inside me.

She knew.

Oh frick, she knows.

I kept my face calm. "What's up?"

She beamed at me, grinning so big that her hair covering pressed into her cheeks. "The annual Hunter Society Gala is coming up."

I nodded, feeling relieved she hadn't started with *Did you allow Prince Luka to feed from you and are you now imprinted like werewolves?*

"I always take a senior hunter with me to represent the Spokane branch. I'd like to bring you."

Holy bloodsucker.

My mouth opened and closed like a fish as pride

and shock ripped through me. Did this mean … I was a senior hunter? "Thank you, Maz … I'd be honored."

Every branch of the society all across the world sent a lead member like Maz and one senior hunter to the gala. It was a huge freaking honor to rub shoulders with the society's elite.

She nodded, smiling. "We leave Friday. Pack an evening gown. If you don't have one, buy one. You could meet your future husband at this thing." She winked.

Maz was badass, and in some ways forward thinking, I mean she was one of the founding members of the society, but in every other aspect she was old school. I was nineteen! Marriage was so far off my radar it wasn't even funny.

"I'll get a dress. Thanks." Friday was three days away.

"Hey, Maz … does this mean I'm a senior hunter?" I was still in shock by her invite to the gala.

Maz walked over to her desk, using her key to unlock the top drawer. My breath hitched in my throat as she pulled out the twenty-four-carat golden stake pin and handed it to me. "Wear it with pride, dear. You deserve it."

As I reached for the pin, a small pang of guilt

washed over me. I technically hadn't killed Luka Drake … but I could have, and I watched Thorin die, so there was one less Drake in the world.

Yeah, I did deserve this.

I ducked out of the office with a smile on my face.

"She asked *you?* What the hell? I'm basically her daughter." My bestie crossed her arms and glared at me from behind the punching bag.

I chuckled, throwing a right jab into the bag as she reached out to steady it. "Way to take the high road and be happy for me."

She blew air through her lips, staring at the golden pin I had clipped onto the top of my sports bra. Today after I got in, I'd showered and crashed I was so exhausted. This was my first time seeing Liv. I'd woken late this morning to an empty apartment, and after I'd put makeup over my neck bite, and read a bit of the *Hunter Scriptures* to reinforce the fact that

I still hated evil vampires, I'd gone in search of my bestie.

"Obviously I'm happy for you. But … I thought we'd make senior hunter together." She pouted, pushing her thick bottom lip out.

Liv was so gorgeous, I swear I felt like a beast next to her sometimes. She was a curly-haired hazel-eyed goddess with full lips and curves in all the right places, and she knew it too. I felt beautiful, but more in an exotic way, a way that not every guy liked. I was half Singaporean, half Sicilian-Italian according to my adoption papers, and I often wondered about my birth parents.

"Hello? Welcome to Earth?" Liv waved frantically in front of my face and I threw a left jab.

I shrugged. "Sorry, babe. I'm just that good."

After flipping me off, she changed the subject. "Hey, I had an idea while you were sleeping. Just to make sure that thing we talked about earlier is really a myth."

The color drained from my face and I looked over my shoulder. We were in the training room doing high intensity workouts. My bright red hair was plastered to my neck with sweat, covering the feeder marks. The marks were almost gone. Within another twenty-four hours they should be unrecognizable.

"Okay…" I thought we'd agreed to forget about it. That it wasn't a big deal.

"Come on, I'll show you." She started to unwrap her gloves. Our workout was over, but we usually showered after and then grabbed lunch from Kenz. This must be damn important to bring her sweaty, hungry ass off schedule. As we weaved in and out of hallways and up the elevator of the society, it dawned on me where we were going.

"The Creepy Library?" I whisper-screamed.

She looked back at me, grinning. "Remember when we came in here when we were like thirteen? They had that freaking preserved vampire finger in there."

I remembered. She'd run back to the youth dormitory shaking in fear. As Liv got to the double doors and placed her finger on the keypad, it beeped, letting her in.

There was a regular hunter library with normal books and stuff, and then there was this thing. This was … more like a relics vault. We all called it The Creepy Library, even Maz, who I was pretty sure named it. Anything weird that we found while hunting, like a pendant or vampire appendage, made it in here. Not to mention a boatload of rare books stolen from the bloodsuckers themselves.

I wondered if Liv thought we would read about vampire imprinting in here … assuming it was real.

"You're a genius," I told her as we entered the stale smelling room. I would surely put this fear to rest by finding a book in The Creepy Library that said it wasn't possible for a human and a vampire to imprint.

She grinned and both of our gazes fell on a jar with a petrified bat inside.

"Eww." Liv squirmed and reached for a book that sat just behind the bat. One by one we just grabbed books and flipped through them, looking for anything having to do with imprinting or mental speak. I was reading a book on vampire royalty and their powers when I stilled on the family tree.

Luka Drake.

My fingers brushed his name and I wondered if my blood had saved his life. He seemed pretty damn alert and healed as I was leaving…

Under his name was his birthdate, 1989. Weird, he was thirty-two. I mean, he looked twenty-two, but they all did unless they wanted to allow themselves to age more. At least he wasn't one of those nine hundred year old ones. *Those* freaked me out.

Under Luka's birthday were two words.

Dominus coercere.

My hands froze.

My Latin was impeccable. Those two words basically meant "master of compulsion."

Everyone in the royal family was rumored to have one special power, and most of them could compulse, which luckily we were immune to as hunters—part of the genetic upgrade we had. Maz did say that it would take the queen herself to be able to force a hunter to do anything, but … what about a master of compulsion…?

Did Luka … use it on *me*? Did he do things and make me forget them? Oh my … a sick feeling rushed through me but I had to push it down.

No. He wouldn't. He wasn't like the others.

"Find it?" Liv looked up from her book and I snapped mine shut.

"Nope."

I couldn't even process this compulsion stuff right now. I just wanted to keep looking for more information on imprinting and forget I ever saw those two words.

After two hours, the grumbles of our stomachs forced us to go down to the cafeteria and get whatever was left over from Kenzley's amazing lunch buffet.

As we turned the corner to the hunter cafeteria, Ricky Vasquez turned as well, nearly plowing into Liv. When he saw her, the smile slipped from his face.

Ric and Liv had been on-again, off-again dating since they were fifteen, but each time got more serious and they stayed together longer, making the breakup all the more painful. This time they'd been together two years and Ricky said he wanted to marry her before we found him screwing Daisy Hawkins in the rec room. He said her wanting to stay a virgin until marriage was too hard for him to handle.

Asshole.

"Olivia." He used her full name, jarring me, because she was Liv to me.

"Vasquez." She nodded professionally, continuing to walk right past him.

His hand snaked out and grabbed her upper arm. "Wait, can we talk?"

Her head snapped to the side and she stared at his hand on her arm. "Don't. Ever. Touch. Me. Again."

His face fell and he let go as Liv stormed off. I

repositioned my walk to be closer to him. "Hey, dirt-bag," I muttered, and smacked my shoulder into his as I blasted past.

If you cheated on my best friend, then you were dead to me. There was no getting back together this time and I hoped he knew that. Vasquez said nothing, just watched as we walked away with his head hung low.

As we entered the cafeteria, Liv made a weird noise in her throat. A yip of surprise. I turned to her and noticed the shock marring her features.

"It's a day for ex-boyfriends I guess," she said, and I followed her gaze.

I scanned the crowd to see who was here, and my throat tightened a little.

Sterling.

Liv stepped in front of me, as if she could shield me from the fact that the love of my life was a mere twenty feet away. She searched my face for any indication of alarm, but I just smiled and smoothed my sweaty hair down, because he had already seen me and there was no leaving now.

"I'm fine," I whispered, and she nodded curtly, moving to the side.

Sterling got up from one of the ten banquet style tables and walked over to me casually, like he didn't throw my heart into a blender six months ago and move to New York City. I tried and failed not to let my eyes roam over every inch of him. When God made Sterling, he spent twice the time he did on creating me. The man was perfection. On a scale of one-to-ten, Sterling was an eleven: a pretty boy with perfect teeth, bronzed skin, blond hair, and piercing green eyes. Even his damn jawline was sexy. There wasn't an inch to pinch on that man, he was all chiseled granite, rock hard.

"Hey, Aspen." His deep voice caressed my skin like an old friend as I shook myself out of the trance he'd put over me.

Sterling was my first love, first kiss, almost my first everything. I'd wanted more out of our semi-casual relationship and his answer was to break up with me and move to New York. He lived in a New York City society house now, and had a new girlfriend from what I'd heard.

"Hey. You're in town?" I tried to act nonchalant, but my hand shook a little as I reached for the pita bread and hummus that Kenzley offered me on a tray he was carrying. What law made you always run into your ex when you were dressed like a sweaty pig?

"Yeah, chasing a mark that fled," he said casually,

and reached onto my plate, grabbing a grape and popping it into his mouth like old times. I wasn't sure if I loved the fact that he'd just done that or hated it.

I think I hated it.

"Those are fun," I said. You got free first-class airfare on the society's dime and got to hang with new hunters out of town. We had a society house in every major city in every country. My dream was to check out the Paris Vampire Hunter Society house one day.

There was an awkward silence and Kenz cleared his throat beside me. "Miss Aspen, I have taken the liberty of ordering you three evening gowns for the Hunters' Gala. They will be delivered to your room by this evening so you can choose your favorite."

God bless you, Kenzley. He was trying to make me look cool in front of my ex. He had done no such thing, because he knew I'd order my own dress.

"Thank you," I told him, and he bowed slightly before walking away.

Sterling's eyebrows lifted. "Wow. Maz is taking you? Senior hunter, then?" He sounded shocked. His gaze flicked down to my chest at the pin that was tacked on to my sports bra and I tried really hard not to stick my boobs out … and failed.

Anger bubbled up to the surface at the disbelieving tone in his voice. "Yeah, is that hard to believe?"

He bristled. "No … I—"

"I just had a tough workout too, so I'm gonna run. Good to see you." I waved him off as Liv grabbed two turkey sandwiches and we beelined it out the door.

"Good to see you!" he shouted after me.

Screw you, dude, I wanted to call back, but didn't. It was good to see him in a bad way. A way that was painful but felt good. I probably needed therapy. He was an asshole, not as bad as Vasquez but emotionally unavailable, and I'd ignored that for too long.

"We need to date normal guys. The society inflates their egos. We need like … engineers or bankers, or boring guys who think we are exciting," Liv declared.

I laughed. "I'd like to see you date a freaking banker."

She was right though. Men in the society were notoriously full of themselves and emotionally unavailable. I just needed to focus on my work and forget all about any men in my life.

"HOLY SHIT!" Liv shook my shoulders, pulling me out of a deep sleep. As my eyes snapped open, a headache slammed into me. I groaned, rolling onto my side, feeling like my tongue was swollen and stuck to the roof of my mouth. Staying up until 3 a.m. and watching chick flicks while eating all the candy in our apartment had been a bad idea.

BAD.

"Go away," I mumbled to Liv, and rolled away from her, searching for my water.

"Dude, I couldn't sleep because Vaz was drunk

texting me all night, so I went to The Creepy Library."

I bolted upright so fast I almost knocked into her face. "And?"

Her eyes were wide. "And *if* this is true and *if* you did do this … you're totally screwed." She held a ratty brown suede book in her hands.

"Liv!" I looked at my best friend, horrified. "You're supposed to ease me into it. What does it say?" I stared at the book, my heart in my throat.

Liv chewed her lip. "It's bad."

Oh Lord, help me. She didn't know how to be a best friend, clearly. I was going to have a heart attack over here.

I ripped the book away from her hands and split it open to where her thumb had been marking the spot.

Imprinting

Only werewolves imprint.

"Oh thank God, Liv, you scared the crap out of m—"

"Keep reading." She winced, perched on my white comforter with red cherry print. I looked down at the book and went on.

Vampiric imprinting, unlike werewolf imprinting, can only be done with a willing

feeder and it is very rare. The vampires call it the Bonding. It is not a process one can control, but is thought to be born out of conditions with many factors.

1. The vampire and feeder must both be sexually attracted to each other.

Frick.

2. The vampire must be near death.

Double frick.

3. It must be the first time the vampire had fed from said feeder.

I closed the book and stared at Liv wide-eyed.

"Keep reading," Liv urged me. "Its gets worse."

I wasn't sure what could possibly be worse than the knowledge that we had in fact fulfilled all three criteria for vampiric bonding, but I pressed on.

The first case of vampiric imprinting is well documented. The vampire and feeder imprinted and then slowly learned the grim reality of their new future together.

Oh no. Oh God, help me.

The vampire can never drink from another feeder (including animals) again without it tasting and acting like a poison to his/her system. Only the imprinted feeder's blood will satisfy and keep that vampire alive.

The room swam as dizziness washed over me.

The feeder takes on the vampire's symptoms of thirst until that vampire's thirst is quenched. The symptoms are headaches, nausea, thirst, and rage.

I stilled. Headaches, check. Thirst, check. Nausea, check.

About to be in freaking rage mode … check.

Finally, all that is known of the vampiric imprinting process is that the vampire and feeder can share thoughts, form an extremely close bond, and will be that way until death. If the vampire dies, the feeder can live on so long as they regularly bloodlet to reduce platelet buildup. But if the feeder dies, the vampire will expire from thirst or poison trying to quench said thirst with outside blood. This is a magical and lifelong bond in which the feeder's body begins to make more blood to feed the vampire regularly.

That was it, I couldn't read any more. I closed the book and stared at the wall. Shock settled into my entire being as I sat there, frozen and unable to move or think. I just breathed, in and out, in and out.

"Aspen?" Liv rubbed my back. "Do you feel … any of the symptoms?"

All I could do was nod as a single tear ran down my cheek.

I was bound to Luka Drake for the rest of my life. Or his life…

Hadn't the book said if he was killed I would live on just fine? All I'd have to do was donate blood regularly…

It was like lightning struck from the sky and I stood.

Praise God.

I charged into my bathroom. "I know what I have to do."

"What!?" Liv called outside the door, as I started to run the shower.

"I'm going hunting!" I shouted. I was going to finish this job, end this *bond,* and move on with my life.

"Are you sure about this?" Liv followed me toward the door. My hunter bag was slung across my shoulder.

I glared at her. "Since when do you protect bloodsuckers?"

She shook her head. "Not that. About going alone. I can totally help you. Make sure it gets done. Hell, if it's hard for you, I can do it myself."

I shook my head. "No, this is something I need to do." This was a mess I'd gotten myself into, and Luka was a strong royal with compulsion. I couldn't let Liv get hurt. She didn't seem convinced.

"I'll be fine," I told her, wrenching the door open to find a sleeping Vazquez curled in a ball at my feet.

"Gross. Does he seriously think you'll take him back?" I peered at the piece of crap who'd broken my bestie's heart.

Our talking had stirred him. He bolted upright, wincing as he grabbed his head. Funny how the male hunter code of conduct conveniently left out drinking and sex. "Liv, baby, I messed up. Let me come in and talk."

My bestie glared at him and then flicked her eyes up to me. "Call me if anything happens. I can meet you at the ice cream place." She winked.

I nodded, brushing past Vaz, making sure to knee him in the collarbone as I passed.

"It's over. I'm too good for you," Liv told him, and slammed the door behind me.

Girl power, I mentally sent to my bestie as I traversed the halls of the society. Liv was one of the strongest women I knew. I loved that she'd had the balls to do that.

"Going hunting?" Maz's voice made me jump

three feet into the air and I grasped my chest, spinning in her direction.

A nervous laugh escaped me. "You scared me."

She didn't say anything, eyes on my hunting bag, awaiting an answer. Maz was loving, a grandmother figure, strong woman of God, but sometimes she could be scary.

"Nah, I'm going to get my blades sharpened." I thought quickly, rattling off an answer as to why I would have my hunting bag. Every three months, we all went to a special bladesmith in the city and sharpened our weapons and got new razor wire loaded. I was due next week but could go early to cover my tracks from today's festivities.

She seemed satisfied with that, giving me a small smile. "Oh good. Ready for our trip? Get your dress?"

The dress! Maybe I would need Kenz to send three dresses for me to pick from. "Yep. Ready and excited." I bopped nervously on my heels.

"Listen, I know you and Sterling were an item, so I think it only fair to warn you he will be accompanying us to the gala as leader of our security team."

I frowned. "Security? We're both hunters, we don't need security." I laughed. The idea *was* laughable. I could bring Sterling to his knees if I wanted, so could Maz. Now it was her turn to look nervous.

She glanced left and right down the hall, before approaching me. Stepping closer, she leaned in and lowered her voice to a whisper: "I have it on very good authority that one of our lead hunters is in bed with the vampires. There may be an attack enroute to the gala to wipe us out, and I want to be fully prepared in that case."

My eyes widened. In *bed* with a vampire? Attack to wipe us out? "Who?" I croaked.

She shrugged. "Someone in our Chicago cell we think. Best to play along until we have proof, then we'll take care of them."

Take care of them? Someone goes "to bed" with a vampire and she kills them?

I swallowed hard. I was so screwed.

"Right. Sterling. Won't be a problem, but thank you," I mumbled.

Spending a weekend trip with my ex was the least of my worries right now.

She nodded. "Carry on. Tell Rufus I said hello."

Rufus, the blade maker. *Right.*

"Sure thing."

Could this day get any worse? I didn't want to tempt fate by asking.

After frantically dialing Rufus and asking him to squeeze me in for a last-minute blade sharpening a week early, I found my way back to the apartment building Luka had been holed up in. My symptoms were getting worse: headache like my brain was being split in two and mouth so dry I thought I might die of thirst. The fact that I was feeling *his* symptoms was totally horrifying to me, and I couldn't wait to kill him and be done with this evil magic bond he'd conned me into. I was going in there guns blazing, taking Luka out and then heading to Rufus' shop in case Maz checked up on me to make sure I really went. Then I could put this whole thing behind me.

Forever.

I'd run out of his apartment so quickly I hadn't thought to look at the door number, but I did remember going down four flights of stairs. Or was it three? My hand was on the door that was the entrance to the side stairwell of the apartment, when his voice invaded my head.

'Aspen?' It was weak but there, and it brought with it a whole host of emotions and feelings that nearly sent me to my knees. How the hell did he

know my real name? I'd introduced myself as some made-up name I didn't even remember right now. Did he read my mind? That made me shiver.

He was hurt. Thirsty. Poisoned. In pain. In need. I *felt* this.

Good, this would make my job easier. I wrenched the door open and took the stairs two at a time. The closer I got, the more I just *knew* his location. It was unsettling as hell. We were connected … and that horrified me.

As I neared his door, the thirst I'd experienced this morning hit me full force. So did the headache right at the base of my skull. This was *not* okay. I should not be feeling things someone else was feeling. It was wrong.

When I jiggled the handle and found it locked, I knew I had seconds to act before he got the strength to fight back. I needed to be quick about this. *Walk in, take off his head and be done.* With one super charged kick, the door splintered open. I strode inside, slamming it behind me, and followed my intuition as to where he was. I was being pulled to him like a magnet. Passing the couch where he'd first fed from me, my stomach warmed at the memory, but I pushed it aside.

Demon magic.

I went back to the bedroom, and that's when I saw his legs peeking out from behind the bathroom door. Pulling out my katana, I steeled myself, pushing the door open wider.

When my gaze fell onto his body, crumpled on the floor, I faltered.

Luka looked up at me from where he lay on the tile floor surrounded by black, bloody vomit. "Aspen … I knew you'd come back for me," he whispered, teeth chattering.

I froze. His voice … was so tender. The way he said my name was the way you'd speak about a beloved. It … gave me pause. This wasn't a hissing creature from hell trying to kill me.

I didn't know what to do with this guy.

The black, bloody vomit told me he'd fed from someone, someone that wasn't me. He was poisoning himself and probably didn't even know it.

I swallowed hard.

I never asked for this, I didn't want this! Holding my sword high, I leveled it over his neck.

"I'm sorry," I whimpered.

He looked up at me with complete and total acceptance in his piercing golden gaze, black at the rim. That's when my eyes fell to one of the many tattoos littered across his body. I stared at the word, "Family," inside of a heart. He was so … human-like.

'Do it. I'm dying anyway,' he spoke weakly into my mind.

I'd killed vampires before, over seventy of them to be exact. In the back, while they were sleeping, while they were screwing, I had no morals about it. A mark was a mark, a vampire was a demon. Evil and without a soul.

But him … he'd saved my life, he'd carried me out of that bar unconscious while he was injured and bleeding and set me in his very own bed. He took off my shoes and laid them nicely against the wall before he collapsed onto the couch and nearly died…

This felt like murder. You couldn't murder a demon, they were evil, so it didn't count, but … Luka, I just didn't sense any evil in him, and my convictions faltered.

My sword clattered to the floor as my throat constricted with emotion.

Dammit!

"Regenerate! You're a vampire, that's what you do!" I screamed at him, even though I knew why he wasn't.

He grasped for me and I steeled myself, thinking

he meant to grab my arm and take my blood by force, but when I crouched down to be closer to him, he took a lock of my hair between his fingers. "I … like … the red better."

What?

Oh, the wig.

This guy was on death's doorstep and he was commenting on my hair?

I sighed, feeling the moment my soul chose the darkness in him over the light of the hunter code. I was probably going to hell for this.

"Go on. It will heal you." I pressed my wrist to his mouth.

He looked up at me, wide-eyed. "How … do you know? I tried a feeder an hour ago, I just got sicker."

"Just do it. Trust me," I said.

I wanted so badly to read his mind, to know what he was thinking right now. Propping up on his elbow, he took my hand, bringing my wrist closer to his mouth. As his fangs sliced into my tender flesh, that wave of pleasure rushed through me, but it was less intense this time, still consuming but not completely. He sucked greedily from me and I watched him, completely enraptured and hating myself. He was the most beautiful creature I'd ever seen. His long dark eyelashes, full, blood-red tinged lips … I could do worse. If I was going to be tied to a vampire, at least he was hot.

Where did those thoughts come from?

Vampires were evil, demons. I felt enthralled. He had me under a spell or something.

Demon magic.

Then I remembered he was a master of compulsion.

My eyes widened as I wondered if I would even know if he used compulsion on me. Why was I doing all of these things so willingly?

"Have you used compulsion on me?" I suddenly spat, accusatorially.

He pulled back from my wrist in shock, licking the two pinpricks of blood there with his tongue; it sent a shot of heat straight to my groin. I growled and yanked my hand from his, folding it into my chest.

He looked better, more alive. There was color to his cheeks and his eyes lost their black edging. He sat up, crossing his arms over his knees and stared at me.

"I would *never* use compulsion on a woman like that. Ever," he said through clenched teeth, as if I'd accused him of rape.

The weird part was I *felt* the truth in that statement.

"You're different from your family," I observed.

He stood, slowly, and went over to the sink, before proceeding to brush his teeth. I just watched him, like we were some couple who were dating and brushing our teeth in front of each other was totally normal.

Why am I still here? What the heck am I doing?

When he was done, he turned and faced me, looking tired. "Maybe that's why they are always trying to kill me. I am too modern for this monarchy."

Damn. I thought of Morgana, his aunt, and how she'd been the one to hire the Shadow Bloods who'd tried to kill us. I would need some serious therapy if my own family put a hit out on me. That was majorly messed up.

He eyed my blade on the ground and I bent down, picking it up and sheathing it.

I cleared my throat, standing. "We need to talk."

I had the distinct feeling he didn't know what we were. Or I was. Or whatever this bond thing was.

He looked down at his chest as if in awe of his sudden strength and health, then his gaze snapped to me suspiciously. "Why don't I feel like death anymore?"

I swallowed hard. "Yeah, about that..." I don't know why I brought the book, but I'd slipped it in my hunter bag. I pulled it out, opened to the pages I'd read, and handed it to him.

"What's this?" he asked and glanced down. The moment his eyes widened, I knew I wouldn't need to explain any further. "Oh," he said, and then stumbled out of the bathroom, holding the book open as he read. I followed him as he stepped into the living room and away from the gruesome scene in the bathroom. As a vampire hunter who regularly beheaded people, blood and guts didn't faze me, but it was nice to be out here and not reminded of the fact that I'd just let him feed from me for the second time. He finished reading the page and then closed the book with a hard snap.

"Well..." He rubbed his face and then looked up at me. "I thought this was a myth."

"So it's real? I'm ... we're ... *bonded?* Forever?" I swallowed hard.

He cleared his throat, raising his arms above his head and hooking them behind his neck, giving me a full view of his shirtless chest.

"Do you own t-shirts? Because if we are going to

come to some arrangement, then I'm going to need that put in there," I growled.

A halfcocked grin slowly pulled at his face and my legs nearly melted, unable to hold up my body. If Sterling was an eleven, Luka Drake was a twelve.

No. I sent up a quick prayer to be protected from his demon magic, but I was starting to question if magic was afoot, or just a really good looking guy.

"So, we have an arrangement?" he asked, raising one dark eyebrow.

"Maybe." I crossed my arms and glared at him. Maybe if I threw more anger at him, it would stop the fire building inside of me.

"Why didn't you kill me?" he asked suddenly.

"Why did you pull me into the rafters, and then carry me back to your place when you were injured?" I shot back.

"Touché." He released his hands and cleared his throat. "Okay. If you're going to be my full-time feeder, I'm going to take care of you."

What were those stupid butterflies doing in my stomach? He didn't mean *take care of me*. He meant take care of my blood, or pay me, which was all gross.

Get it together, Aspen.

"I'm fine. I don't need you," I snarled. I couldn't

discount the fact that my symptoms had gone and I was feeling better, but that only served to make me angrier.

He just glared at me; one second he was on the couch and the next he was in the kitchen, pouring a glass of orange juice.

Fast bastard. When the glass was full, he walked it over to me and extended his arm.

Rolling my eyes, I appeased him and took a big swig. "All better."

He shook his head, zooming back over to the kitchen and pulling out a bag of frozen spinach and a fresh steak.

I pointed to the spinach. "Keep dreaming, bud. Mac and cheese and donuts are my jam."

"I don't want you getting anemia." He threw the spinach and steak in a skillet like a male Martha Stewart.

Put a freaking shirt on!

"I'll take iron pills." I crossed my arms. "Besides, the book says I'll make extra blood to feed you."

After placing some garlic and other seasonings in the pan, he threw a lid on it and then turned to face me.

He stated the obvious: "You could kill me at any moment and move on with your life."

"I'm not a murderer."

He smirked. "Really? What are those notches on your blade, then?"

I looked down at my kill count carved into the wooden handle and rolled my eyes. "That's different. These demons are rapists and murderers, they got what they deserved."

Luka blew air through his teeth. "I forgot how uber religious you hunters are." He pointed to my rose thigh tattoos. "House of Rose?"

I squirmed under his gaze. I didn't like being called *uber religious*, and I really didn't like someone knowing what hunter house I was with. How did he know House of Rose was the religious house?

I tried to change the subject: "So, how often do you need to feed. Bare minimum?"

Was I seriously even entertaining the thought of working out a feeding schedule with this guy?

He chewed on his bottom lip and I forced myself not to think it was sexy. I needed to get out of here. *Now.* "Every forty-eight hours to sustain life. Twenty-four hours to keep up my strength, and twice a day to thrive."

Thriving sounded a little excessive.

I stood, slinging my hunting bag over my shoulder. "Forty-eight might work for me. I'll see you in two days." I turned to leave.

"Wait! Your steak."

I waved him off. "I'll take vitamins!"

I'd just agreed to be Prince Luka Drake's feeder. God help me.

I spent the next day in a flurry of packing and training and getting ready for the society gala. So much of a flurry that I'd totally not planned for one very important thing.

Luka would need to feed while I was gone…

Frick.

I'd gotten my blades sharpened and bought two killer dresses. We left for Portland in the morning for four days. Even if I fed him tonight, he'd die while I was gone.

Maybe that was best … maybe cutting off his head was too hard for me because it felt like murder, but killing from thirst while I wasn't there wouldn't really be blood on my hands, right?

Except the memory of him looking up at me from the bathroom floor, asking me to put him out of his misery, had burned into my brain. Then he'd made me spinach and steak like he cared…

He did care. *About my platelet count.* I needed to keep reminding myself of that!

A genius idea came to me then.

Grabbing my coat and cell phone, I flew out of my apartment and headed for Luka's place. This idea would change everything.

As I turned the corner, passing the hunter library, I slammed into someone's chest.

"Shoot, sorry." I backed up and looked to see who I'd collided with.

Of course it was my ex-boyfriend, because that's exactly what I needed right now.

"Sterling. Hey."

He was rubbing the spot on his chest where my face had smacked. Being five-foot-four and dating a guy who was over six feet tall had its challenges. "In a hurry, Aspen?"

Man, I'd missed his deep, gruff voice.

"Yep. See ya." I stepped around him, then his arm came out and gently grasped my hand.

"Hold up, Rosie." He rattled off his pet name for me like it was no big deal and my stomach dropped.

I froze, looking up at his beautiful face. What's with ex-boyfriends? Why did they get ten times hotter the moment you broke up?

"What's up?" I tore my hand away from his, hating that I missed his touch. Sterling was a commitment-phobe and I wanted marriage, a house with a white picket fence, and two kids. We were bound to break up eventually, I just needed to get over it.

He looked down at me. "Why do I feel like you're avoiding me?"

Oh for Pete's sake, he wasn't this stupid, was he?

"Because I *am*." I crossed my arms and he frowned.

He looked offended. "I thought we were cool."

"We are. I don't wish you were dead, but I don't want to have coffee and talk about our hopes and dreams," I informed him. "That's what being cool is about."

His frown depended. "You're still pissed at me for leaving?"

I chuckled. I'd forgotten how clueless and stupid Sterling was when it came to matters of the heart. "What do you care? I told you that I was in love with you and you moved across the country. End of story. Now enjoy your new life and leave mine alone."

I brushed past him but couldn't help glancing over my shoulder to see the hurt in his eyes.

"Aspen, wait! It wasn't like that."

Liar. It was exactly like that. He tried to position it as a "job transfer" that had magically come up the day after I told him I loved him, but it was all bullshit. He told me he wasn't the committing type the first time we'd kissed. I should have listened. Picking up my pace, I didn't stop, I just continued to plow through the House of Rose like hell on wheels. I was not going to let Sterling mess up my already complicated week. I just needed to get through the gala and then he'd run back to New York with his new girlfriend.

Stepping outside, I walked two blocks to where my yellow Beetle was parked, then I turned off my phone in case the society had GPS'd me, and slipped my repaired watch into the glovebox, making sure that was off too. As I was heading over to Luka's apartment, questions spun in my mind. How long could he hole up in that place without his psycho family finding him? I wanted to know what Maz was talking about when she spoke of a rumored drama in Magic City and what he did to get into jail.

Also, why was his own family trying to assassinate him?

When I got to his door, I banged a few times, really loud, like a cop would. Vamps slept in the day, so it would take something loud to wake this dude no doubt. I could … feel him, just beyond the door. Even after only twenty-four hours apart I had the mild headache, thirst, and agitation symptoms of needing to feed. They were manageable but annoying.

The door wrenched open and my breath caught in my throat.

Luka stood there shirtless, low slung silk sleep pants barely hanging onto his hips. Silk was like the thinnest material *ever* and only served to outline every inch of him … it hid nothing.

I gulped.

"Aspen?" He seemed confused. "I thought you would be by tomorrow. Come in."

Standing back, he let me in and then shut and bolted the door behind him.

"Yeah, sorry, I have a trip coming up. We leave early tomorrow so I need to do … this … today."

"A trip?" He frowned, reaching up to rub his tousled hair.

Put a freaking shirt on, dude! I could barely focus

on my words. Was he carved from rock? God help me.

I started to have inappropriate thoughts, like could vampires have sex with humans and did they shoot blanks, and immediately shot those thoughts down.

Focus.

"Yes, a trip! I'll be gone for four days. We can feed today and then you can draw my blood and drink that while I'm gone."

I puffed out my chest at my ingenious plan.

"Four days!" he shouted, rubbing his face. "That won't work."

He walked over to his kitchen island and picked up a book. It was brown suede, identical to the one I'd brought.

"What's that?" I played dumb.

He handed it to me. "You left it here. It seems you stopped reading before the good part."

Left it here? Damn, I hadn't even noticed; the one page was enough to do me in. I scrolled past the stuff I'd already read.

One final mention. In a bonded pair, the vampire must never drink the feeder's dead blood. It acts as poison and will kill them.

That's the part I missed?

Awesome.

"Dead blood?" I queried.

"Bottled. Bagged."

I cursed. "I have a life you know. I can't just be at your beck and call like a blood whore!"

He flinched. "I would *never* call you that."

'Ever,' he sent mentally.

The sincerity of his words caught me off guard. I could feel his emotions and it was weird. He felt … normal. Nice. Sweet. Not a douchebag vampire.

"Look I have to go to this thing, okay. I … didn't ask for this bond with you. I'm doing the best I can to keep you alive, but it's starting to get complicated and we are only on day three."

He stared at me, making me squirm. "You act like *I* did this on purpose. Like I knew what I was doing. I thought imprinting was folklore. *You* offered your blood to me and I took it. Now *we* have to deal with it."

I felt like we'd created a baby together and were now fighting over how to raise it. I raked my fingers over my face and then crossed my arms, looking up at him. "Well, I can't miss this thing."

He nodded. "Very well. I think that's fair enough. Where is it? I'll travel with you."

My eyes bugged. "Travel with me! Hah. No, that would get us both killed."

He seemed to understand. "Ah, a *work* thing, then?"

The way he said work, there was definite shade thrown. "Yes, a *work* thing. It's in Portland."

He nodded. "I'll travel separately there and text you my hotel information. You can come to me at your leisure."

Sneak away at the freaking Hunters' Gala?

I guess that could work…

"Okay, fine. Then feed today so I only have to feed you once on my trip." I didn't really see an alternative.

Because I'd decided I couldn't just let him starve, right? I already felt his crappy hunger symptoms and it sucked. I felt bad for leaving him like this for two days at a time.

"Aspen?" The way he said my name made my legs go a bit weak.

When I looked up, he stepped closer to me. "I never got to thank you … for saving me. For coming back each time."

Sexual tension charged the air then, pressing against my chest like a tangible object. It was so thick I had to step backward in an effort to break it.

"Yeah well … you're decent," I straightened my shirt, "and I'm not a murderer."

That was a foggy statement but all I could muster.

He nodded. "So, we should probably exchange phone numbers…"

He pulled out his phone and I fumbled for mine. "Right."

You've sucked my blood two times, so yeah now is a good time to get my number.

I put his number in my phone under, *Random Dude From Bar*, just in case he called while other people were around. I could play it off that I had a secret boyfriend or something.

"Here's a key, you can quietly let yourself in." He handed me a silver key to his apartment. "I have roommates, but they're in Vegas right now. I'll let them know about you though so it's not weird."

My eyebrows rose. Okay, that was probably a dig at my banging on his door while he was asleep, but whatever. Did I need a key to his freaking place? I dated Sterling for two years and didn't even know his phone password, much less have a key to his apartment. Luka's hand was outstretched still and it started to get awkward, so I just grabbed it from him and shoved it in my jean shorts' pocket.

We stood there quietly, knowing he still had to drink from me.

"Did you get those vitamins?" he asked, honey flecks dancing in his blue eyes.

I shifted on the balls of my feet. "I'll get around to it." I shoved my wrist at him. "Might as well drink now, so I don't need to worry about it tomorrow while I'm traveling." I repeated my earlier statement, wishing he would just get it over with.

The day after tomorrow was a training session, and then that night the big gala. I'd have to pop over to his hotel in the morning so that there was no chance Maz got tipped off to his presence at the gala that evening. I was already stressed just thinking about it.

He nodded, stepping forward and grasping my wrist lightly in his hands. When he brought his lips to my skin, pleasure spread up my arm and into my chest.

I tried to suppress it, to push it back, but I couldn't.

What is this? I'd been fed from before, and what they said in movies about it feeling all euphoric was kind of a lie. Vampires did emit a small amount of drug to make you feel good, but if you knew what they were, you also felt grossed out, a bit like an animal being fed from. This wasn't that.

This *was* euphoric. This was yummy, this was…

Before I knew what I was doing, I'd stepped closer and tucked my body right into his, pushing my hips into his pelvis. He looked up at me, eyes flashing gold, hungry. But not for my blood. He stopped drinking, licked the wound, and never took his eyes off of me.

We were inches apart and I hadn't moved back. I just stared into his eyes as bright copper threaded through them, and for some reason seeing my fresh red blood on his lips turned me on. It was like I'd claimed him, like he was mine.

I shook my head, repulsed at those thoughts, and it was like coming out of a daze. I stumbled back a few paces.

"Are you using compulsion on me?" I asked, bewildered.

He looked at me like I'd slapped him. "Never. I told you. I won't do that."

I placed my hand on my hips. "Why not? Why didn't you just use it that night the Shadow Bloods attacked to make them go away?"

He scoffed, and I was very aware that the bastard still hadn't put a shirt on. "It doesn't work like that. I can use it with one person here and there, but a group, or in an attack … it depletes my energy."

I frowned. "Well, I would think in a life or death situation you could have used it on those Shadow Bloods!"

His face drew into an angry expression as he scowled. "I could have, but then I wouldn't have had the strength to carry *you* home with my intestines hanging out!"

Oh, so it's my fault?

"Why *did* you carry me home?" I shouted.

This had turned into a full-on argument. His fists were clenched and my chest was heaving, but I just didn't care. I wanted to hate him, I wanted to see him as an ugly person, because the alternative was too much for me to handle.

"I don't know! Clearly that was a mistake!" he yelled.

Now it was my turn to clench my fists. "I should have taken your head at that club!" I bellowed.

We stared at each other, chests heaving in frustration, which was comical since vampires didn't need oxygen.

Then his eyes fell to my lips. "I made a split decision to save the pretty girl. *Don't* make me regret it." He spun and started to walk back to his bedroom.

"I'll see you in Portland!" he called out behind him, slamming the door.

"Hah! *You* saved *me?*" I hurled at him in fury.

Okay, technically he did, but my ego was bruised and this mother effer was going to learn just how badass I could be.

After I stopped staring at his ass…

Luka Drake had gotten on my last damn nerve. I should have just let him die. It would have been a lot easier.

I WAS ALL PACKED. Fancy dress, check. Skinny jeans and cute top for networking, check. Hunting bag in case shit went awry while away, check. Senior hunter pin affixed to the top of my thigh-high boots. Check. Check. Check. I was going to the freaking Hunters' Gala and I couldn't be more excited!

"Stop grinning like a fool." Liv tossed the kitchen hand towel at my face.

I tried to wipe the smirk off my face, to no avail.

"I'm going to be among legendary hunters. This is a *huge* honor."

She nodded. "With Sterling and your imprinted vampire in tow."

"Shhh!" I hissed. Even in the privacy of our own apartment I didn't want to talk about *that*. I'd told Liv everything that went down at Luka's and how we'd agreed to have him tag along for the trip. She'd just facepalmed the entire time and then offered to kill him for me.

As she sprinkled more parmesan on her pizza, my phone buzzed with an incoming text.

Random Dude From Bar: Just checked into the Duniway in Portland. Presidential Suite. Key for you at desk.

Damn, the Duniway was a nice hotel and just a few blocks from The Heathman, where the Hunters' Gala was being held. Bold of him to stay so close to where over two hundred hunters were about to be gathered. If he was seen … he was supposed to be dead.

Me: Don't leave your room. My boss thinks I killed you.

Random Dude From Bar: Yes my lady.

"Eww, he's so charming. That's weird." Liv spoke from over my shoulder and I jumped.

"Don't read my texts!" I shouted, clutching my chest. Then I quickly deleted the text exchange in case someone went through my phone.

Liv was frowning, staring down at me with a wild look in her eye.

"What?"

"He's evil. A creature placed on this Earth to tempt you, Aspen." Liv looked at me like I'd slept with him or something.

"I know that!" I screamed, suddenly feeling defensive. "I've read the *Hunter Scriptures* more than you have!"

She recoiled as if she'd been slapped and I softened my tone. "He's different, okay? He saved my life. What kind of evil demon does that?"

Liv chewed her lip. "Maybe you're right. Just … be careful, okay? I don't like this."

I nodded, stepping up to pull my bestie into a hug. "I'm so glad I have you to talk to about this. I feel like I'm going crazy."

"You are," she said flatly and then chuckled. "But I've got your back and I think you *are* following the moral code of conduct … for now. He saved your life and that's good … until it isn't. His true colors will show and then we will take him down together. Okay?"

Her surety that Luka was evil and would someday turn on me made me sick to my stomach. Was I totally being brainwashed and deceived? He'd said he hadn't used compulsion on me, but that could be a lie.

Those thoughts spun around my head until Sterling knocked on my door, prepared to accompany me to the Hunters' Gala.

Why was he wearing the powder blue shirt that he knew I loved? Why was he sneaking casual glances at my lips when I wasn't talking? Most importantly, why did the universe hate me!?

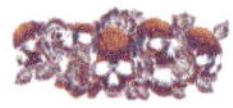

IT WAS a five-hour drive to Portland, six with traffic. Maz sat up front with Finneas while Sterling and I sat in the back row. Two more SUVs full of security trailed behind us. I was still tripped up on Maz's comment that someone in the hunter force was "in bed" with the vampires. What did that mean exactly? And why was she worried about being attacked herself? Traffic downtown was bad, but we finally reached our hotel just before dinner.

The second the driver put the car in park, Sterling jumped out and ran over to my door to open it. Finneas did the same for Maz, handing the key to the valet.

I rolled my eyes at Sterling. "I can get my door, thanks," I told him curtly.

He tapped his chest with pride. "Head of security."

I snort-laughed, touching the pin at the top of my boot. "Senior hunter."

He growled low in his throat. "I missed your fiery personality."

A pang of sadness twisted my gut and I trudged up the steps to where Maz and Finn were waiting. If Sterling and I were broken up, then why did it feel like we had unfinished business? Some random passersby looked at Maz's modest priestess robe with raised eyebrows. It was very similar to a nun's habit and only worn by God's most beloved and chosen in our society.

"Come, Aspen, I think we should check in and then read the scriptures before dinner."

I nodded, jogging to her side. "Yes, Maz."

Just before we stepped inside, my eyes flicked down the street in the direction of the Duniway Hotel. Knowing Luka was so close unnerved me. I'd skip his feeding tonight and then slip my security detail tomorrow morning and feed him before anyone was even awake.

When I awoke the next morning, I felt like I was walking on a cloud. Even though I was having some of the feeding withdrawal symptoms through Luka, nothing could spoil this day for me, because last night at the Hunters' Welcome Dinner, Ruby freaking Thorn sat next to me.

Ruby was a legend from the House of Thorns. The Thorns were known for being … more liberal in their beliefs. They still thought vampires were evil but they didn't follow the extreme rules we did and they didn't read the *Hunter Scriptures*. Ruby was the lead hunter of the society in Spokane for the Thorns, and had the highest kill record on file, even beating Maz.

Me: And she touched my arm when she was grabbing her dinner roll!

I texted to Liv.

Liv: Blah blah stop bragging!

I grinned, sitting up and rubbing my face. It was 6 a.m., but I wanted to get over to Luka's before anyone noticed I was gone. Brushing my teeth quickly, I threw my hair up in a topknot and grabbed my *Hunter Scriptures*. In the off chance I saw anyone on my way out, I would tell them I was going for a prayer walk. Walking around the city and praying that it be rid of demons so that God could bless it was common in our beliefs. No one would question it.

Slipping into my boots, I opened the door to my hotel room and stepped outside, coming face to face with Maz.

I nearly screamed, only able to swallow the sound at the last minute.

"Maz!" I clutched my chest.

She looked startled as well, *Hunter Scriptures* in hand and fully dressed in cream priestess robes.

"Aspen, where are you off to so early?"

Was that accusation in her tone? My heartbeat picked up as I raised my scriptures. "Prayer walk."

Her face softened. "Oh, child, you are one of the most devout hunters we have. Bless you. I'll join you."

Frick.

"Great," I said, trying not to let my voice show my disappointment.

She linked arms with me and started to walk. I had no choice but to go along. I guess feeding Luka would have to wait until later.

There was a sudden movement to my back and I flinched, tearing my arm from Maz and spinning. Fist raised.

Sterling stood there, fully dressed with a katana at his hip as he trailed Maz and I.

"Announce yourself next time. I nearly broke your nose," I growled at him.

"I would have blocked it," he said flatly.

Bastard.

Maz grinned, clearly enjoying our little display. "Prayer walk, children. The Lord depends on it."

Now Sterling was coming! I was sick of seeing my beautiful ex's face all the time, but I'd told Maz it wouldn't be a problem, so I needed to suck it up and deal.

"Yes, Maz," I said as I trailed behind her, keeping one eye on my super sexy ex-boyfriend who needed to book the first flight back to New York City ASAP.

When we reached the lobby I was surprised to see so many hunters already awake and bustling about. They had coffee cups in hand, some from the House of Rose in other countries and states were reading scriptures, and some were dressed in full battle gear. I recognized the House of Ashes logo on one hunter's jacket. House of Rose were the founding fathers of the society and most loyal to God's mission. Next was the House of Skulls; they were pretty devout in the hunter faith but didn't have priests and priestesses like Maz. House of Thorns and House of Ashes were more relaxed groups. They wanted to fight evil and avenge the families who were wronged by the bloodsuckers, but didn't care much for the scriptures.

Maz got pulled into a conversation and I waited patiently for her. There was an entire day of classes and meetings today before the big gala tonight. I had a few classes ticked off on my schedule that I wanted to attend. I glanced down at the list.

Knife Throwing with Ruby Thorn
Water Combat with Master Rain

"Aspen?" I was pulled from my thoughts by a familiar voice.

Turning on my heel, I faced Ruby. She wore her full black hunter gear complete with Kevlar body armor and House of Thorn logo at her breast.

Holy shifter, she knew my name!

Would it be too weird to ask for an autograph? Yes … it totally would. Instead I was just going to geek out that she knew my name.

"Ruby Thorn." I said her full name like an idiot. "I mean hi, yes, I'm Aspen." If you were an orphan adopted by the society as most of us were, you took your house as a last name.

"My senior hunter was injured in practice and I was wondering if you were available to help me demo knife throwing skills later for a workshop I'm leading? Maz speaks so highly of your skills." She beamed at me, tossing her inky black hair over one shoulder.

My mouth went dry with shock as my gaze flicked to Sterling, who was grinning. He knew how much I looked up to Ruby. My knife throwing was decent, but nothing near her level. I wasn't going to turn down this opportunity though. I'd rather lose a finger.

"Absolutely. I'd be honored."

She grinned. "Great, I'll see you at eight? We can practice the basics before the workshop starts at nine."

Two hours.

I just nodded, unable to contain myself. With a wave goodbye, she left and I jumped up and down, silently hand flapping before pretending to faint, throwing myself at Sterling. He caught me, amused, and I burst into giggles.

"Ruby Thorn wants me to co-workshop with her! What planet is this?" I asked him.

He was holding my elbows, looking down at me with a tender expression, and I suddenly realized I'd just slipped back into old times. I'd forgotten we weren't dating or that he had a girlfriend and had stomped all over my heart.

"Sorry." I yanked myself back, wiping the smile from my face. "Got excited."

Sterling watched me with a solemn face, his "I'm too hot to show emotion" face. One I loved and equally hated.

"You should be excited. It's a great honor." Sterling's voice was deep and low and I tried not to pay attention to the way it made my stomach do flip flops. "Aspen ... I left because—"

"Oh look, Maz is ready," I interrupted, and beelined it over to the priestess.

I had enough on my plate. Listening to Sterling talk about why he'd left me after I confessed my love was not something I could handle right now.

Shit. Shit. Shitty shit.

The gala was in an hour and it lasted until midnight. If I didn't go and feed Luka right now, I wasn't going to be able to at all and he would probably die. Besides, I felt like absolute crap. My head throbbed, my mouth was as dry as the Sahara Desert, and I was about to rip someone's head off with anger.

My phone buzzed.

Random Dude from Bar: I feel like I'm dying FYI

Crap. It was his fifth text of the day.

Me: Me too. The day got crazy … I'm coming now. I just need to sneak out.

Random Dude from Bar: Cool, my two friends are here. Werewolves but very cool. You'll like them.

I nearly choked at reading those words. Cool werewolves? I'd like them! Werewolves might not be evil by my standards, but they were … unnatural in

God's design … and I was glad I wasn't tasked with disciplining them like some of the other orders around the world were when they got out of hand.

I walked over to my hunter bag and pulled out two silver stakes. Reaching up under my black dress, I slipped them into my thigh holster and pulled on my stiletto boots. As a woman who was five feet four inches, I needed all the height I could get, and the tips bonused as a killing weapon. If Luka or his friends got out of hand, I'd end them and feel zero guilt.

My long red hair was curled into ringlets, and the upper half was braided over my shoulder. The dress I'd chosen wasn't exactly hunter modesty code, but Maz didn't seem to mind if the younger girls showed their body a little. Controlled rebellion she called it, and a good way to find an interested husband she would say.

The black silk material hugged my frame before slightly poofing out at the waist like a princess gown. The top part was a corset bodice that laced up the front and squeezed my tiny boobs together to make some semblance of cleavage.

Liv and I laughed sometimes at how opposite we were. Where my hair was straight, hers was curly, where my skin was fair, hers was bronzed, and where I was flat, she was curvy. Yet none of that made her less of my sister.

"I got this," I told the mirror by the wall, and slipped a decorative silver cuff over my right wrist that would hide the marks I was about to put there.

My hand stilled on the knob as I prepared what I would say if Maz or Sterling were right outside this door, but when I pulled it back, I was alone.

Thank God.

Slipping out into the hallway, I took the stairwell down to the ground floor, and then burst out the exit door that led to the side alley of the hotel. There was a waiter wearing a dirty white apron, smoking a cigarette, but other than that I was alone.

Giving him a smile and a wave, I booked it for the Duniway Hotel, all the while trying to convince myself that I was doing the right thing by keeping Luka alive.

God, if you want me to stop, give me a sign, I prayed.

As I turned the corner, a redheaded chick a few years older than me popped off the wall she'd been leaning on and waved me down. "Aspen?"

What the…?

I just nodded and she smiled, pulling out a card key. "I'm Sage, Luka's friend. He told me to wait for the other smokin' hot redhead and bring you up to the room."

Smokin' hot redhead? I doubt he said that.

I relaxed a little, and then eyed her with scrutiny. "Werewolf?" I raised an eyebrow, inhaling. Something smelled different about her, but I couldn't put my finger on it.

She nodded, winking.

I waved her off, looking at the key. "I can make my own way up."

"He said you'd try to ditch me." She grinned as we started to walk and I threw a glance over my shoulder to make sure I wasn't followed.

She stepped closer to me and lowered her voice. "There are a few hunters staying at the hotel, overflow from the booked conference. Luka arranged for you to take the freight elevator near the kitchens so you wouldn't be seen."

Oh. That could be a problem, especially since I'd just taught a class and now everyone at the conference knew who I was. That was actually very thoughtful of Luka...

I simply nodded and she led the way, walking two paces in front of me.

I was following a werewolf into a vampire's hotel

room to let him feed from me—what the heck had become of my life?

We slipped down the alleyway and then Sage, my new werewolf escort, pulled open a door that had been propped ajar with a stone. Stepping inside, I heard the bustling sounds of a busy kitchen. Paying them no attention, Sage slipped to the right, down a hallway where a young man no more than seventeen was waiting by a freight elevator. Sage traced a finger across his chest. "Thanks, doll."

The teenager looked like he was going to faint at the attention of such a beautiful woman and merely nodded, holding the doors open while we stepped inside. As soon as they shut, Sage hit the button for the penthouse floor.

With a slight jerk, the elevator whirred upward and I swallowed hard.

"So you hunt vampires?" Sage said as if we were making casual conversation.

I gulped, trying to decide what to say.

"Me too," she added. "We just got out of a year-long war with them. Nasty little bastards."

I frowned. "But … Luka is your friend?"

She nodded. "Well, he's not like the others. Obviously. He helped us win the war, freed our people."

Right … okay … the werewolves had been at war with the vampires. I had no idea.

"How did he help you? I heard he was in prison?" I couldn't help but pepper her with questions while she was willing.

Sage inclined her head. "Yeah he was. But me and my bestie broke him out and then he helped us kill his aunt, the queen. Now we're all on the run from the Magical Creature Council in Magic City."

My eyebrows hit my hairline.

Say what?

The queen of the vampires was dead!

Holy hell, that was *huge* news. No wonder his family was trying to kill him. Drucilla Drake was the most God-awful vampire alive, if reports could be believed, and if Luka helped her reach her demise, then maybe … in some weird way … God wanted me to help him and that's why he'd brought us together.

I relaxed a little, feeling better than I had in days about my decision to keep Luka alive. For now.

Following Sage out of the elevator, I traversed the hallway to an opulent open doorway. Two male voices could be heard as we rounded the corner.

"No way! You remember that brawl differently than I do. I totally had Sawyer!" Luka's voice carried into the hall and I stepped inside of a richly decorated hotel room to see the male vampire casually leaning across a bar top, talking with a handsome but gruff looking male, werewolf I assumed.

The werewolf laughed. "Bro, you were all but crying for release—" The male stopped when he saw me, and Luka's head slowly turned in my direction. When his eyes landed on mine, they hooded as he raked his gaze over my corseted dress.

I swallowed hard. "Food delivery." I raised my wrist and then laughed nervously.

Sage chuckled beside me and walked over to the male werewolf, pulling him in for a light peck on the lips.

"I'm Walsh, Luka's bodyguard," the male said, and Luka rolled his eyes.

"I hate you," Luka growled, but there was a playfulness to his tone. These guys had history.

Luka pushed off the bar and zoomed toward me in a blur, using his vampire speed. My breath hitched in my throat as he was suddenly before me, nostrils inhaling my scent. "Shall we go into the bedroom?" he asked in the most tempting voice I'd ever heard.

Bedroom. Vampire. No.

God help me. Seeing him joke around with his friends made him seem so … normal, and I had to remind myself that he was a vampire, a Drake, no matter how different he seemed.

He was the enemy. Right? *Right?*

"Okay," I squeaked.

He stepped across the room and then opened the bedroom door, gesturing that I go first. I walked over to the bed and then thought better of it, pivoting to the window which had a small, padded bench in front of it. Sitting down, I smoothed my dress and stared up at him.

He looked different, pale, eyes darkened. He was hungry, I realized.

"I'm … sorry if the one feeding every two days is … uncomfortable for you." I felt bad now knowing that he was suffering because I didn't do daily feedings.

He slowly stalked over to me and sat next to me. "I've had worse."

That surprised me. "A Drake has gone hungry? I doubt that." I laughed. The Drakes were the richest vampire family alive. They could afford a billion feeders around the clock.

His eyes grew even darker and narrowed to slits. "You don't know anything about me, so stop pretending that you do."

I reeled back as if he'd slapped me; anger pushed

up inside of me so fast I felt like it was going to boil over at any moment. How dare he? *I* was the one keeping him alive.

"I know enough to know that I should have killed you when I had the chance," I said, thinking of the story Maz told me the night she'd given me the assignment to kill Luka. He killed a woman ten years ago.

Was that hurt crossing his face? It was there for a moment and then gone, replaced by bitter anger. He turned to face me, eyes blazing yellow. "You hate it when anything makes me less of a demon in your eyes, don't you?" He leaned closer to me so that our faces were mere inches from each other. "Well, I've got news for you, Aspen *Rose*. If God made you, he made me too."

My jaw hung open at the blasphemous sentence he'd just said. *If God made you, he made me too.*

How dare he compare himself to me, an innocent human. How dare he sit so freaking close that I could smell his musky cologne and yummy vanilla chapstick.

"Vanilla," I panted, losing track of my thoughts.

He frowned. "What?"

I shook myself, leaning forward to smell his lips.

When I got a few centimeters from his mouth, he froze.

"You're wearing vanilla chapstick. Interesting choice for a guy," I teased, trying to shake some of this stupid tension with a joke. Why were we always fighting? Always hot and cold. Hadn't I just decided in the elevator that God sent me to him? Why did I still want to kill him every time I saw him?

He looked at me with hungry eyes, his fangs distending past his bottom lip. "It's Sage's. My lips get chapped when I'm not fed properly," he snapped.

Not fed properly, as if that was *my* fault. Ungrateful bastard!

"Everything about you repels me!" I growled, suddenly annoyed we'd even talked at all.

"Well, everything about *you* lures me in!" he shouted back, anger running across his face.

"Then take your meal and be done!" I hurled at him, the words barely leaving my lips when he reached up and grabbed the back of my neck, pulling me onto his lap. One second I was sitting on the bench and the next I was in his arms, legs dangling over the side of his as he tipped my jaw up and sank his teeth into my neck. There was no time for me to direct him to drink from my wrist, because this was already happening and holy hell it felt so good I didn't want him to stop.

A moan slipped from my lips as I reached out and grasped his bicep, letting my nails dig into the hard meat of his arm. He yanked my hair a little as he fisted it at the nape of my neck, and heat blossomed between my legs.

This wasn't a feeding to keep someone alive. This was … sexual and wrong, right? He was … bad. So why did it feel so good? Why did he have to say that God made him and why had Sage told me he'd helped save the wolves and kill the evil vampire queen? This was too much. I couldn't handle feeling this way about Luka. I pulled back from him, jumping up to stand, panting as I stared at his wild eyes and bloodstained lips.

"I think you got enough," I squeaked. "And from now on, we need to hide the bite marks."

Luka hadn't moved, he just sat there like a statue, staring at me with glowing eyes. His tongue slowly trailed along his lips. "Oh, I can think of a dozen other places to bite you."

My stomach dropped and a pulse pounded between my legs.

No.

This was wrong, this was against everything I believed in.

"I'll see you back in Spokane in two days," I retorted, and then spun on my heels, booking it out of his hotel room like a bat out of hell.

Something fundamental was happening inside of me, a fissure to my very own soul. The beliefs, the bedrock that I'd built my entire life upon, were shaking, and I didn't know how to stop it before they cracked right in half.

Either Luka was evil or he wasn't, and if he wasn't, then my whole life was a lie.

I made up my mind then. Luka was sent from the devil to tempt me, and when we got back to Spokane, I'd ask Maz for time off. Liv and I would go on vacation for a week and I'd let Luka starve to death. I didn't have it in me to kill him firsthand, but I couldn't do this anymore. It compromised every belief I had.

But one thought looped on repeat while I ran back to the Hunters' Gala: *If God made you, he made me too.*

That couldn't be true … right?

The second I got back to the hotel, I slipped through the busy entryway and ran upstairs to make sure my neck bite was covered. Two puckered scabs stared back at me as shame burned in my cheeks. That was … like a kiss … like how I imagined kissing Luka would feel like. Not that I imagined that. Ever.

I put makeup over my marks, then a small piece of Band-Aid tape I'd cut off. Then I wore a black velvet choker and finally I laid my red curls over that. Overkill? Maybe, but in a room with over two hundred hunters, I wasn't taking any chances.

There was a knock at the door and I pulled in a

deep breath. Walking over to the door, I opened it, preparing to see Maz.

The sight of Sterling standing there handsomely, wearing a charcoal-gray suit, with his light blond hair slicked back, made my heart leap into my throat. His eyes roamed over my dress and a sudden idea possessed me.

"Aspen." His voice was husky as he tipped his head to me. "Maz is already downstairs. I thought I would accompany you."

Without giving it much thought, I stepped forward and crashed into him, wrapping my hands around the back of his neck and pulling his lips to mine. His body went rigid with shock beneath me for the slightest second until he sprang into action. He reached out and wrapped his hands around my back as he pressed me harder to him and I opened my mouth to deepen the kiss. When our tongues collided, he let out a moan.

My thoughts were so frantic, I was so hellbent on trying to prove to myself that I had zero sexual feelings for Luka, that I couldn't even focus on this kiss with Sterling. It was mechanical, fake, not *real* in a sense. I'd kissed Sterling hundreds of times, but this felt different, this was … a mistake.

I pulled back, my fingers going to my lips in

shock. I couldn't believe I just did that, that I'd pulled Sterling into this just to deal with my own issues.

"I'm so sorry … your girlfriend…" I felt so stupid.

Sterling stepped closer. "Ex-girlfriend. I'm leaving New York, Aspen. I'm moving home. I want *you*." He reached up to cup my chin and his fingers brushed under my choker and against my bite marks and the Band-Aid there.

He frowned. "What happened?"

Frick!

"Curling iron." I stepped back. "We should head down to the gala."

"Aspen, I just told you I was moving home and I want you back." He looked vulnerable for the first time in forever and I felt so guilty I wanted to cry.

What was I supposed to say, *I actually just kissed you to prove to myself I wasn't developing sexual feelings for a vampire?*

"I … need to process that. We should head down to the gala," I told him again.

He nodded, seeming to get the social cue that I wasn't interested in talking or touching anymore.

"Can we talk about this when we get home?" His voice held such vulnerability that it pinched at my heart. I'd known he had commitment issues when I started dating him, I just thought I would be the one to fix him. Every woman probably thought that about their man's issues. Maybe I would have enjoyed that kiss more if my head wasn't such a jumble.

"Sure. When we get home." I gave him a slight smile.

He seemed to relax at that and then stepped up to my side, extending his arm. "Shall we?"

I slipped my hand into his, all the while feeling like an imposter in my own skin, and put on a fake smile.

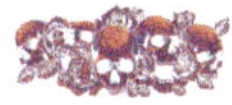

Maz introduced me to everyone. I met hunters from Canada and Mexico. Not to mention the food was amazing. This entire conference was the highlight of my year. My gaze flicked to the wall where Sterling and a few other hunters chatted as I licked the remnants of chocolate cake off my spoon.

I felt off emotionally and wondered if I was having a mental breakdown or something. My entire life I'd seen all vampires as evil demons from hell and spending time with Luka was making me question that. I didn't want to question my reality, I wanted things to just stay the same as they had always been. Safe and easy.

Without warning, Luka's voice boomed in my head. *I'm sorry about before. That was ... inappropriate of me.'*

I froze, eyes widening as I looked around the room, as if a bunch of human hunters could tell I was mentally talking to a vampire.

'Where are you?' I hissed.

'In my hotel room.'

'And you can talk to me?' This was bad, so bad; we were two blocks apart. Shouldn't that ... I dunno, break up the signal?

'I think every time I feed, our bond gets ... stronger. I feel some emotions from you as well, to be completely honest.'

Oh, Lord, kill me. Embarrassment flooded my system. *'Well, don't be so honest, then. I'm just having a weird time. My ex-boyfriend, Sterling, is here and it's awkward.'*

I felt sharp jealously spike through my chest for a split second and then it was gone. *'Well. Have fun. I just wanted to apologize if I made you uncomfortable.'*

The mental link went dead and I felt an emptiness in my chest for a second, followed by guilt. Why had I told him I was with Sterling? Just to see if it would affect him? What was wrong with me? It *had* affected him though. That's what that feeling in my chest was … that jealousy was his.

"Seat taken?" Ruby's voice said from beside me.

I snapped my head to look up at her and grinned. "No."

She was wearing an elegant and revealing red gown, with her black hair braided over one shoulder.

Ruby looked across the hall at Maz, who was speaking to another House of Rose member, and then focused back on me.

"Do you like being at House of Rose?" she asked suddenly.

I frowned. "Yeah. I just made senior hunter." I beamed.

She nodded, giving me a small smile. "Congratulations. Well, if you ever decide you want to go somewhere … more freeing…" She eyed my black velvet choker and I paled. "I'd love to welcome you to the House of Thorns. We may not be as devout, but we do feel strongly about justice and righting the wrongs the supernaturals have caused."

What was she saying? House jump? That was so rare and super frowned upon. Hunters had a shelf life anyway. Most didn't make it past their thirtieth birthday, and we were as die-hard about sticking with the house we were born into, as someone would be about a football team.

Ruby looked across the room and fidgeted nervously. "Well, I gotta run. You know where to find me."

She stood, walking to the back wall where the refreshments were.

I followed her gaze and saw Maz walking toward us, a scowl on her face.

Did Ruby Thorn just try to poach me?

I … I didn't even know what to think about that, but my first thought was that I would never leave Liv. Ever.

I chewed on a fingernail, replaying the part where she'd eyed my neck choker, when someone screamed, "Bloodsuckers!"

For a trained hunter, it took me way too long to process what was happening. I spun slowly, mouth agape, as dozens of vampires zoomed into the giant ballroom, crashing into tipsy hunters dressed in their best attire.

I felt frozen, staring at the attack and wondering how … why? Was this what Maz warned me about?

"Aspen!" Sterling's shout broke the spell over me

and I snapped into action. Reaching under my dress, I pulled out the two stakes I'd stashed there earlier in case Luka or his friends tried to kill me. I popped up onto the tabletop, my boot knocking over two glasses of champagne just as one of the vampires reached Maz.

The sixty-five-year-old priestess opened her mouth and hissed at the demon as she yanked a razor wire from inside her robes. My gaze darted in every direction, trying to see who needed my help the most. This wasn't like a vampire attack on a bar, which happened often and the main objective was to protect the weak humans. The people these blood-suckers were attacking here were trained hunters. Albeit most of them were drunk...

My gaze darted back to where Ruby had gone to get a drink. A vampire charged at her, and she took the stem of a champagne glass, snapped it off, and shoved it into the vampire's eye.

Holy crap. It was mayhem.

I glanced at Sterling, who had his katana out, full on beheading the bastards left and right, but there were so many I could barely track what was happening. They just kept coming, which meant that Maz was right: one of the hunters was in bed with a vampire and gave up our location. This was a planned bloodbath, all in an effort to take out our top ranks.

Not on my watch.

A figure zoomed bedside my table, going right for a human waiter, when I leapt off the top and jumped onto his back. My arms hooked around his neck and he leaned forward as if to bite my wrist, but I'd already rammed my stake into his heart, right through his back between the fourth and fifth ribs. I jumped off of him as his body started to decompose—these stakes weren't laced with the preserving serum.

I yanked my weapon out and spun, ready for the next.

Oh, God, help us.

They just kept coming. Their sheer numbers dwarfed us, and I felt defeat settle into my bones.

'What's happening? You feel ... terrified?' Luka's voice boomed in my head.

'We're under attack. Your good ol' buddies are about to exterminate my people,' I growled at him, unsure why I was placing blame on someone who had nothing to do with this in the first place.

"Aspen!" Maz shouted, and I turned just as a female vampire slammed into my chest. I was launched backward, sailing through the air, and landed hard on a chair. A scream ripped from my throat as one of my ribs cracked. I sucked in a breath, only to regret it once my broken rib expanded.

Get up! I told myself. *Hunters die on the ground.* I didn't plan on going out like that. The female who'd chucked me was gunning for me, blasting through the place with her curly brown hair trailing behind her.

Ignoring the pain in my ribs, I popped to my feet, stakes in each hand.

"Let's dance, demon!" I snarled as she skidded to a stop with a feral grin. She inhaled, and then something in her face changed—confusion set in, then disbelief.

"You smell of a Drake." She barely got the words out when I charged.

Running full speed, which was about half of what a vampire could do, but way faster than a human, I held my left stake hand low and my right stake arm high. This way I could stab her if she dropped to the ground or tried to jump over me.

She hissed, jumping up to go high, and tried to kick me in the face, but I was ready. With my right stake I stabbed her in the abdomen, and my left stake sank into the meat of her thigh. Using all my modified DNA strength, I yanked her down and she slammed into the ground, hard. I was about to remove one of my stakes and pierce her through the heart, when Sterling's katana came down on her neck, removing her head.

I looked up to find him covered in blood that didn't seem to be his.

"Thanks," I panted, and Sterling growled, looking over my shoulder.

There were more. Way more.

My gaze flicked to the two exits signs. Five vampires were posted in front of each. They were blocking us in. Those bastards. This was a bloodbath.

"New mission. Take out the demons at the exits, give others a chance to escape," I told him.

A hardened look came over Sterling and he nodded once. We weren't all making it out of this alive. That cold, hard, fact had settled in.

"Retreat!" I called out in the loudest voice I could muster over the sound of my fellow hunters getting slaughtered. It's like I'd woken them from a dream. One by one, the hunters must have realized there were too many. We were bred for war, born to fight, but sometimes you had to live to fight another day. The injured and alive started to work their way to the exit doors just as Sterling and I reached them. Maz and Ruby were fighting back to back, and if I weren't in total survival mode, I would have been in awe because it was a sight to behold.

Sterling shoved his sword at me. "Take my katana."

"No!" I pushed it back, holding up my stakes. "I'm fine."

He snarled, but he knew better than to tell me what to do. Reaching down I pulled the caps off the ends of my stiletto boots to reveal the small, spiked stakes there. I had to keep the weight on my toes so they didn't get stuck in the carpet, but I was ready to party now. The heel stakes rarely got use, and if I was going to die tonight, I was going to go out in style, after sticking one of these in the neck of one of the bloodsucking bastards.

With a battle cry, Sterling and I ran forward, attacking the five guards at the left exit door with precision and unyielding fury.

I slammed the stake of my left hand in one of their chests just as the other wrapped his fingers around my throat. Reaching up with my left leg, I threw a high kick into his ribs and grinned when the heel stake entered his flesh. He stumbled backward with a shout and we pressed on, moving them away from the exit doors.

"Aspen!" Maz shouted and I used one second of my free attention to glance at her. She was in the open exit doorway, helping others escape.

"Go!" I shouted, looking back at the advancing vampires and then back at my mentor.

She stared at me with sorrow and pride in equal measure as the realization that I wouldn't survive tonight settled into her.

"God bless you and keep you!" Maz shouted, her voice cracking with emotion.

My throat tightened, but I didn't allow myself to get overwhelmed. Tears meant blurry vision and blurry vision meant death, so I pushed everything back down and pressed on, pushing the vampires back with Sterling and a few others. We wouldn't win, but we would keep the majority away from the exit doors to allow our hunters a chance to escape.

The problem with pushing the vampires away from the exits meant we had backed them into a corner and now our backs were exposed to the open room. I felt the warmth of a body approach me just as the vampire in front of me lashed out and raked his long fingernails across my face. A second later, something sharp ripped through my back and a bloodcurdling scream tore from my lips.

I looked down, shocked to see a wooden stake had been driven into my abdomen from behind.

"No!" Sterling yelled, but as he tried to reach me, two vampires took him down, one of them wrestling his katana away from him.

This was it. This was the moment they prepared you for in the society. The moment you would meet your maker and hope that you had done all you could in life to make him proud. I just hoped I had served him well, doing my best to fight evil at every turn.

I spun, wanting to face my attacker and not die in fear with my back turned to the one who would grant me death. When I did, I came face to face with an old-ass vampire who looked like he wanted to swallow me whole.

I raised my arms, hands shaking as the shock of my wound set in and I realized I wasn't even strong enough to drive this stake through him.

The old man grinned, peeling his lips back to expose his teeth, and I readied myself for death.

Lord, have mercy on my soul. Make it quick, I prayed.

I was about to close my eyes and give in to the

dizziness washing over me when a blur of move-ment, faster than anything I'd ever seen, slammed into the old man and he went flying. I started to fall, my legs growing too weak to keep me upright. Luca zoomed into view and reached for me. I landed in his arms as he drew me to his chest, face looking as pained as I felt. Sage and Walsh, the two werewolves from his hotel room, were in their wolf form, tearing into vampires left and right.

I looked up into Luka's stormy eyes. "You came for me?" My voice was breathy, weak.

Luka frowned, staring down at me with tender-ness. "If you could stop trying to get yourself killed, I wouldn't have to."

I smiled weakly at his joke, but my eyes crossed as I tried to focus on his beautiful face.

"You need a healer." His voice held a sudden urgency.

He moved to leave but I cried out, "My friends!" I looked over his shoulder to see Sterling fighting for his life as he snuck shocked glances at me. He was probably wondering why I was draped half dead in some vampire's arms. One of the wolves trotted up to me, and by the smaller form and rust colored fur I imagined it must be Sage.

"Please help him. Help my friend." I gestured to Sterling.

Without another word, Sage and Walsh took off, darting through the melee and pouncing on the back of the vampire attacking Sterling.

Luka's fingers gently probed my wound and I whimpered, my teeth chattering. "It doesn't even hurt anymore," I assured him.

His jaw clenched. "That means you're near death. Pain means you're still alive."

With that sobering fact, everything blurred around me as he zoomed us out of the gala, and then the dizziness finally took me, and everything went black.

Muffled voices pierced the blackness. I tried to focus on them, but it felt like I was drowning in cold darkness.

"Drive faster!" Luka's voice snapped, panic and tension registering in his tone.

Luka.

Memories suddenly came rushing back to me, the gala, the attack. *He saved me, he came for me.* I was totally wrong about him, I could see that now. Maybe all of the other vampires were evil, but not him. He was good.

"I'm going as fast as I can without wrapping this car around a pole," a familiar male voice called back.

Walsh. The werewolf.

Arms tightened around me and I forced myself to open my eyes. Luka was holding me firmly to his chest. We were in the back seat of a car as Walsh drove us and Sage sat shotgun. Sage had a phone pressed to her ear. "Yes, she's bleeding out, and if she dies, Luka dies too. She's his only food source now that they've bonded."

Her words tore into me like a thousand blades.

Luka was working so hard to save me because I was his food…

Bile rose in my throat, and he looked down at me then, shame coloring his pale cheeks when he saw that I was awake. I closed my eyes, not wanting to deal with the reality of what was happening here. I was falling for a vampire who was fighting to keep me alive so he could have dinner.

My eyes sprang open and Luka opened his mouth to speak.

"Sterling?" I rasped, and Luka's face darkened.

"They got him out." Luka nodded to Sage and Walsh.

My eyes started to un-focus and I shook my head slightly in an effort to fix them. "I…" I didn't have the breath to speak, and I couldn't feel my body anymore. It's like I didn't have a body, which was weird.

"Don't talk." Sage flew into the back seat, straddling the center console to put her fingers to my pulse. "It's weak but it's there," she told someone on the phone, and then pulled it from her ear, looking down at me. "We've got the alpha's surgeon flying in via helicopter. You're going to be okay."

Alpha surgeon? As in Alpha werewolf? What the…? Maybe I hadn't heard her right. We generally were not permitted to go to hospitals as our accelerated healing would tip them off that not all was right with the world. But we had some of the best doctors in the country on the society's payroll … just not here right now. Portland would have had a medical safe house, I just had no idea where it was because I hadn't planned on being attacked while here!

The car skidded to a halt and then I was moving. The door opened and Luka whooshed out with me in his arms. Everything blurred, then suddenly we were stepping into a helicopter.

A male doctor wearing full surgical gear put up two blue gloved hands. "Whoa, this is a completely sterile space," the doctor barked at Luka. "Give her to my nurse and go."

I felt Luka's arm tighten around me slightly at the

mention of letting me go. A female nurse stepped toward me with her arms outstretched. Her blue gloves were pulled up over her white gown and she wore a mask and clear face shield so that all I could see were her blue eyes.

My gaze darted around the helicopter. There was a gurney, IV bags, surgical tray…

They were going to do surgery on me in a helicopter!

I inhaled. They were wolves; they smelled like Sage, a smell I hadn't really noticed before but now recognized. Luka was going to leave me with were-wolves to die in a helicopter!

"No," I whimpered to Luka. "Just let me die." If God was ready to take me, then I was ready to go.

Luka pressed me to his chest, looking down at me with wild eyes. They burned with desperation, need, and … something I couldn't identify.

'I can't,' he said, and then deposited me into the nurse's arms.

The nurse had kind eyes and she gently lowered me onto the table.

"You can meet us in Werewolf City," the doctor told Luka, who was standing there, blood covering his shirt as he stared down at me in shock. The heli-copter blades whirred to life, making every tree and bush in the open field sway, and Luka took a step back, nodding.

Werewolf City? "No … I'm human. I can't go there—"

"Don't worry. We are going to take good care of you, dear." The doctor placed an oxygen mask over me and suddenly a sweet smell coated my nostrils and tongue. Heaviness pulled at my limbs as I felt the drugs course through my system.

'No,' I pleaded.

'I'm sorry.' Luka's voice bled through mine and then I let go. I didn't have the strength to hold on anymore.

"IF SHE DIDN'T HAVE regenerative capabilities, she would have died instantly." The male surgeon's voice pierced my brain and my eyelids flew open.

"Regenerative capabilities?" Luka's unique, deep timbre was slightly warbled as the effects of the drugs still left my system.

"DNA modifications. When younger," I croaked.

"Aspen?" Luka called out and I moaned, looking around. I was in a hospital room. The four walls were white and clean, but the door ... was blown off; scorch marks kissed the edges.

I frowned and Luka followed my line of sight before nodding. "War. Werewolf City is only now rebuilding. Are you okay?"

I looked down at my gown and pulled it up to reveal a giant puckered wound with over a hundred stitches. Pressing the gown back over my bare legs, I looked up at the surgeon. He was about forty years old with a little salt and pepper hair. "Thank you," I told him.

I guess God wanted me to live another day.

"You're welcome." He nodded. "You should stay off your feet for a week. I'm still unsure what rate of healing you have, but a week to be safe."

I nodded. Liv, Maz, Sterling ... I needed to get back to the society in Spokane.

I was about to try to sit up when a gorgeous blond walked into the room and grinned at Luka. She was wearing cut-off jean shorts and a t-shirt that said *Fragile Like a Bomb*. Her long hair was braided over one shoulder.

"Can't even stay out of trouble for a week?" she scolded Luka, and then pulled him into a hug.

"What can I say, I missed you guys," Luka told her, grinning as he wrapped his arms around her.

Jealousy spiked through me before a giant male followed in after her.

Holy hell. He was like a tatted-up Chris Hemsworth. This *had* to be the alpha. He reeked of power and … manliness.

"Stop hitting on my wife," the male told Luka in a playful tone as she pulled away from their hug.

Luka shook his head, grinning as the big alpha pulled him into a bro hug and they rapped on each other's backs. "Of all the girls you could bind yourself to, you chose a vampire hunter? Really, bro?" The alpha shook Luka as if that act might shake some sense into him.

I'd forgotten all about my desire to flee, now I was entranced by this little get-together. It was a side of Luka I didn't really see. A side of werewolves I'd *never* seen.

The girl looked over at me and noticed me lying there, watching them. With a soft smile, she approached the bed. "Hey, Aspen, I'm Demi. Sorry the place isn't exactly top notch, but we're working on repairs from what the war damaged." She extended her hand and I took it in mine, shaking it gingerly.

Demi … that sounded familiar. I didn't read much news about the werewolves. We had a weekly newsletter, but I skimmed it for vampire related stuff only.

Demi...

"Oh … Demi." Realization dawned on me as I heard her name. "You're the … you're both." I pointed at her mate. I'd read an article in the society email newsletter that covered their recent wedding. Sawyer was her husband's name. It was of pertinent news to us because they were both alphas, and that might shift the political landscape, which could drive more supernaturals out into the human world.

"Werewolves?" she said. "Extremely good looking?" she added with a grin.

I snort-laughed and then grabbed my side, wincing at the pain. "Alphas."

Demi nodded, trailing her finger across her leather wrist cuff. "I mean technically, yeah, but I'm pretty much in charge around here."

"Hey!" Sawyer growled, causing Demi to grin.

Damn, they were so normal. It was hard not to think of them like me … but they weren't. I liked her but I couldn't stay here. I had to get a hold of Liv and let her know I was alive. No one in the society could know that I was in Werewolf City right now or my career would be over.

"Well, thank you for the help, but I need to get back." I started to sit up, biting through the pain.

"Whoa. Chill. You need to rest." Luka zoomed to my side and started to gently push me back onto the bed.

"Don't touch me!" I snapped at him, and everyone in the room froze.

I looked at Demi and frowned. "I'm sorry. Could I speak to Luka alone please? It was nice to meet you, and thank you so much for your help in saving my life."

Demi nodded, clearly catching on that there was more drama here than she understood, and waved Sawyer out of the blasted-open doorway.

Luka peered over at me like I'd grown three heads. "What's wrong with you? The doctor said you need to stay off your feet for a week."

Sage's words from the car came back to me. Luka wasn't concerned with me, he was concerned over my blood.

"Yeah, I can heal at home. I'm not staying in Magic City with a bunch of werewolves, no matter how nice they seem."

His forehead wrinkled, his eyes narrowing to slits. "Wow."

My teeth clamped together. "Wow, what?"

He shook his head. "I expected a thank you for saving your life."

I scoffed. "Thank you for saving your future dinner," I snapped. "Let's not pretend this is more than that. From now on, I see you at mealtimes and you forget I exist otherwise."

The hurt that crossed his face looked genuine, but he also didn't deny my words. "Sage just said that because—"

"I don't care," I interrupted. "Look … I need to get back or this will be harder to explain later," I told him. "Just drop me off at the nearest bus station or call me a cab."

His eyebrows raised, but then he looked down at me with a flash of anger. "Fine. I'll have Walsh drop you. It's clear you only want to see me as needed. Goodbye, Aspen."

Those two words, *Goodbye, Aspen* tore into my heart way more than I thought they would.

It was better this way. Anger was good. I could handle anger. It was attraction, lust, and the other stuff with Luka that I couldn't even begin to comprehend.

Walsh popped in about ten minutes later with keys in his hand. Sage stepped up next to him and faced me. "The van is all gassed up. We can take you to a hospital in Portland. Your cover story is that a human hotel employee found you bleeding out in the hallway and called an ambulance. You were treated at the hospital and released. You can call your people from there to make the cover story seem legit."

I could tell by the cadence of her voice that she was annoyed with me. Long gone was the nice girl from the elevator. Luka must have said something to her and he must have thought up the cover story, which was actually really good.

But we were in Magic City. It was somewhere in Idaho and over six hours' drive to Portland. I was already feeling so exhausted, I just wanted to sleep. But if they dropped me off at the society in Spokane, Maz would want to know how I got there.

"Thank you," I said.

She nodded curtly, and Walsh just pushed the wheelchair up to the bed as I slowly managed to get myself inside of it and slumped into the seat, wincing every few moments at the fresh waves of pain.

"Ready?" Walsh asked, his voice pretty devoid of emotion. He seemed like the strong and silent type.

I nodded, and Sage dropped a bottle of pills in my lap. "For the pain," was all she said.

Great. These people were nice to me and helped save my life and I was being a total asshole.

Walsh pushed me out of the blasted-open door and I looked to the left, my eyes catching on a bunch of tradesmen sweeping up rubble or painting or repairing glass.

"The vampires did this? In the war?" I asked Sage. "Don't you hate them?" I looked up at her.

She nodded. "But we don't hate *him*." Her gaze went to Luka, who was down the hallway speaking in low tones to Sawyer and Demi as they all glared at me.

Fabulous. I'd just made enemies with the people who'd saved my life. Way to go, Aspen.

I was just too tired to care, and after hearing Sage talk about me as Luka's meal plan, I wasn't too worried about their feelings. It was my own I needed to protect.

Once we got in the van, I lay flat on the back seat, popped two pills, and fell into a deep sleep. I just needed to get out of here and back with my own people. I wasn't used to nice supernaturals. It was throwing me off.

Why couldn't things just be black and white, good and bad? Why did Luka Drake have to be gray?

"I THOUGHT YOU WERE DEAD!" Liv screamed into the phone the second I called her from the waiting room of Portland's emergency room department.

"Me too. Come get me?" I just sat in a van for six hours to get here. I didn't want to drive all the way back to Spokane, but it was the role I needed to play for the cover story. I'd tell Liv everything later, but if she was with Maz, I needed to—

"Aspen!" Maz's voice came on the line, and I was relieved I hadn't said anything about what had really happened. "We've been worried sick. They couldn't find your body and Sterling said he lost sight of you."

Fear spiked through me at the mention of Sterling. He'd seen Luka carry me out…

"Is he okay?" I dodged her question.

"He's recovering but will be fine. Honey, how did you get out?"

My mouth went dry. "A miracle," I said flatly, hoping I wasn't going to hell for that one.

"Praise God," she agreed. "We're on our way."

I'm pretty sure God was looking down at me and facepalming every five minutes, because I was making some pretty epic screw-ups down here.

My week of recovery was the weirdest week of my life. During the day, I lay next to Sterling, my ex who I'd stupidly kissed, as we both mended in the society's healing ward, and at night … I snuck away for feedings with Luka. We both discovered that I was healing faster and felt better with daily feedings as opposed to every two days. Liv helped me get out, under the guise of going for a walk, which was doctor-recommended daily, and Luka would jump out of a library or bookstore or coffee shop and take his meal.

We barely talked, I didn't moan, and he drank from my wrist only. It still felt good, but something had changed between us. This was a business arrangement now, as it always should have been.

Now that I was healed and back on hunting duty, I was ready to slay some demons and live my life. Maz and the rest of the society were on high alert after the attack at the gala—no more hunting alone. We'd all paired up. Liv and I were officially hunting partners until we had more info on who led the attack on the gala and why. Sterling had tried to ask me a few times about the vampire who carried me out and the two werewolves who had helped him, but I told him I didn't remember anything and he dropped it.

Liv and I were going on a raid tonight with a team of other hunters, but I needed to feed Luka before we left. As I was walking down the hallway, Maz turned the corner.

"Oh, dear, I'm so glad to see you up and about again." She beamed at me, her eyes falling to the leather wrist cuff jewelry I now wore almost constantly. "You sure do like those bracelets. I don't understand young people's fashion," she added.

My heart picked up speed and I let out a nervous laugh. "Well, you know me and Liv, we like to keep up with the latest trends. I'm going for a run, and then I'm excited to do that raid tonight."

Maz nodded, clasping her hands in front of her. "Be safe."

As I walked past her, I swear she inhaled as if trying to *smell* something on me. Okay … no more wrist biting. Clearly that was getting suspicious. I'd have to figure something else out.

I drove my Beetle to Luka's apartment and parked two blocks away at a local park, jogging the rest of the way just in case there was a tracker on my car. If anyone asked, I drove to this park to run because it was pretty. When I made it up the stairs, I knocked. It was around 8 p.m. and Luka would be awake. Using the key felt weird, especially since he said his roommates were back from out of town.

The door opened to reveal a tall, lanky male fey. I froze, staring at the tips of his pointy ears, my heart hammering in my chest. The tattoos that crept up his neck screamed danger. Stepping back a few paces, I wondered if I had the right apartment, but I recognized the couch behind him.

"Hello, delicious," the male purred, his blond hair swooping into his eyes as he ran his gaze up and down my body.

I reached behind my back and pulled out my pistol, brandishing it before him and pointing it right between his eyes. "Hi."

The dude's eyebrows hit his hairline. "Damn. You must be Aspen."

I grinned, proud to have that sort of reputation around here.

"Bennet, I presume?" I lowered the gun slightly. Luka told me about his male roommate but had left out the fact that he was a freaking fey!

"Hello," a female purred behind me and I spun, pulling my Glock back up and pointing it right at the girl.

Upon seeing who it was, I calmed. *A little.*

Isabella Drake was even prettier in person than the pictures they showed us at the society.

She looked at the gun in my hand and then at Bennett. Her long black hair hung in inky, glossed curls to her waist. She wore a black leather miniskirt and hot pink lace top with a black bra. "I like her." Isabella grinned, flashing her white sharp teeth in my direction.

Luka strode past Bennet and into the hallway, reaching out and pushing my gun hand down. "Don't worry. I'm eighty-nine percent positive she won't hurt us."

I lowered the gun and holstered it as Luka walked around in front of me.

"Can we take this inside, ladies?" He looked down

the hallway to make sure none of the neighbors were watching.

"After you," I told Isabella.

I wasn't giving this girl my back. I didn't care if she was Luka's roommate and cousin. She was a vampire and I trusted none of them.

She grinned. "Smart girl." Then she gracefully swished her hips as she strolled into the apartment, trailing a finger along Bennett's chest as she passed.

I heard interspecies reproduction was actually possible, but only with the fey. They had super sperm or eggs or something that defied all natural physics and produced a child with any of the races. There was a name for the supernatural mutts, but I couldn't remember it.

I stepped inside and closed the door behind me, keeping my back to the wall so that I could keep my eye on all three of them.

"She's cagey and it's kinda hot," Bennet observed. "Is it true all hunter society girls are virgins?"

My cheeks burned with embarrassment, but before I could tell him to shut his mouth, Luka stepped in front of me. "Bro, she's off limits. Why don't you and Izzy go and watch a movie."

Bennett held his hands up defensively. "Apologies."

Isabella saluted her cousin. "Come get us when you're done. We're meeting Sage and Walsh at that rager later."

Rager? Like a party? I froze. "What rager?"

Isabella curled her upper lip at me and said nothing. Apparently her fondness for me had worn off.

I rolled my eyes, pulling out my phone and rattling off the address to the tip off we'd gotten about the giant vampire party we were going to raid tonight. All three of their eyes widened. "Yeah, that's the one," she said.

I sighed, my internal moral compass starting to spin in circles. "Don't go there."

Luka stepped closer to me, bringing the smell of his yummy cologne with him. "Why?"

Peering up at him, I regretted it instantly. He was so gorgeous it actually befuddled my thoughts. "Don't go there," I repeated, pleading with my eyes. I couldn't tell him any more without completely choosing a side.

He nodded once. "We'll go to Bang."

With that, Izzy and Bennett disappeared into the apartment and I stood there awkwardly. Did I just tip them off that we were raiding their party? What if he called and told all his undead friends not to go anymore? Why was I so stupid?

"Don't tell anyone…" I didn't know what to say.

"Tell anyone what?" he growled. "You haven't even told me anything. You don't trust me or my friends. That's clear."

I liked flirty Luka better than asshole Luka, but that's why asshole Luka was probably better for me. I shouldn't like him at all.

I blew air through my teeth and ran my fingers through my hair. "I'm tired of this, Luka. I don't want to do this anymore."

"Me neither," he shot back, but I could hear the tone in his voice; he was hurt by my admission.

Why couldn't I have bonded with a guy who had a pulse?

Now I felt like an asshole. He'd called a freaking helicopter to save my life, and his friends were really nice to me, and I was just being a bitch.

"Look…" I rubbed my arms, trying to find the words. "This is really overwhelming for me. I've … lived my whole life dedicated to…" My voice cracked. I felt too vulnerable to even be speaking this out loud.

"Killing my kind?"

I swallowed hard. "Yes. Killing your kind. The ones who *rape* and *murder* and drink from humans like soda fountains," I shot back.

He nodded. "There are a lot of bad supernaturals out there, vampires usually being the worst. I won't deny that, but there are a lot of bad humans out there too."

Relief settled into my chest that he would admit such a thing and he was right; the list of murdering and raping humans was quite long. Stepping forward, he approached me, looking me dead in the eye. "But vampires are not all the same. We were not *created* to rape and murder, we were human too once, just like you, until someone changed us."

The realization of what he'd just said hit me like a brick to the head.

Luka Drake was human once... I ... I'd never thought about it like that.

"And not all of us asked for this life. I didn't," he added, a darkness passing over his face.

Holy shit.

What if ... what if some of the vampires I'd killed were forcibly changed? Against their will? I'd never even conceived of the fact. We'd all been told they wanted power and money and status, so they willingly gave themselves, especially the Drake line.

But what if that wasn't true...?

"Luka ... I never thought of that. I'm..." I felt like crying for some stupid reason.

"You're really naive," he stated plainly.

"Hey." I reached out and punched his arm, only to wince as it nearly broke my fingers. Dude was made of stone.

He grinned a little, and Lord help me he was so beautiful when he smiled.

"I'd rather you be naive than a heartless bitch," he said bluntly.

"Too far!" This time I reached up my hand to really let him have it, but he caught it midair, yanking me forward as I stumbled toward him, slamming my body flush up against his.

"And a naive, devastatingly sexy woman with red hair is my kryptonite," he huffed.

All rational thought left my brain then, my faith, my beliefs—they melted along with my resolve. Being this close, having whatever this bond was between us, I could feel him, like *really* feel him. Physically, emotionally, spiritually. Luka was a kind man with a good heart. He was strong and hard around the edges, but with a soft center. He was … I shuddered, my breath feathering over his face as he inhaled.

He leaned forward and whispered in my ear, my wrist still gently clenched between his fingers. "I dream about tasting you."

My heart nearly leapt out of my chest in that moment as my stomach dropped. "You taste me every night," I offered, breathy, trying to regain my composure.

"I don't mean your blood." Luka's lips trailed my earlobe and I pressed closer to him. Reaching up under his shirt with my free hand, I raked my nails down his back.

He moaned in my ear, and in that moment I wanted to strip off every single piece of clothing I had on and give him my virginity. I'd had many hot and heavy moments with Sterling, but I'd always been able to stop things before they got too heated. But with Luka, all of my moral lines stared to blur.

My phone buzzed between us and I jerked backward, ripping my hand from his shirt as he let go of my wrist. My cheeks flushed as I panted, and Luka watched me, unmoving from his place.

With shaking fingers, I pulled out my phone.

Liv: Raid party leaving soon. Where you at?

Me: Be there in ten.

I put my phone in the side pocket of my tiny running shorts. "I gotta get going," I told Luka, trying to forget the fact that I'd almost just kissed him.

He nodded. Something had thawed between us,

we were back to that dangerous place where I felt myself having thoughts I shouldn't have about a vampire.

He extended his hand, asking for my wrist, and I shook my head. "It's getting too obvious. We need to do it somewhere … more discreet."

A sly grin pulled at the corners of Luka's lips. "I love how much humans blush. It tells me a lot."

Kill me now.

I rolled my eyes. "Shut up. Got any ideas?" I pulled up my shirt to expose my stomach. "Here maybe?"

Luka's grin faded, eyes going half-lidded. "As much as I'd like to bite you there, I need a good vein."

Right. Veins. Where did I have a good hidden…

My gaze flicked to his to find him looking at my crotch. Stepping forward, he reached out and brushed a light finger over my inner thigh. "The femoral artery is a good one if … you wouldn't be too uncomfortable with that option."

I swear the lightest pink tone colored his cheeks. "Now *you're* blushing." I couldn't help but smile. I felt like I'd caught him.

Luka rolled his eyes. "Oh please. I can be completely professional about this."

I crossed my arms. "Good. Me too. Clock's ticking. I gotta go. So let's do this."

Even as I said it, nerves bunched in my stomach. Good thing I wore tiny shorts or I might have had to disrobe.

Luka cleared his throat, nodding. "Would you like to come back to my room or…"

I flinched. "No, that would be weird."

"Right. Here, then." He gestured to the living room.

I opened my legs, popping my right thigh to the side as if opening myself to him, and he dropped onto his knees.

Holy mother of vampires … seeing him on his knees in front of me with my legs open made my head swim with desire.

Ignore it, Aspen! It's just their natural charm.

He just sat there, on his knees, staring at my bare thigh.

"Luka?"

Shaking himself, he cleared his throat. "Sorry. Got distracted."

Reaching out, he grasped the back of my thigh with his hands, and then without warning sank his teeth into my inner thigh. A gasp tore from my throat as his warm wet tongue caressed my skin and the aphrodisiac properties of the bite tore through my system.

I'd gotten good at holding back when he fed from me, and he only took what he needed, so it was relatively quick, but this time I couldn't hold back—I didn't want to. I tangled my fingers through his hair, pressing him harder into my thigh as he moaned his approval. Waves of pleasure crawled up my body, mixed with heat and desire, threatening to consume me.

What did it feel like for him? I wondered.

My breaths came out in ragged, short gasps as I heard footsteps behind me.

"Oh damn," Bennett called out, and Luka tore himself from my leg, licking his lips.

"It's not what you think." Luka had the sense to look embarrassed while I just closed my eyes, frozen in mortification and wishing I would disappear.

"It's cool, bro. Do your thing." I could almost hear the grin in Bennett's voice. I wanted to die. Footsteps retreated and I stayed there, eyes pinched shut, still hoping to disappear.

When I finally opened them, I noticed Luka was holding his mouth, trying to keep from laughing. When he saw me, he pulled his hand away and burst into uncontrolled snickers.

"It. Was. *Not*. Funny," I growled, but I was unable to keep the anger in my face as his chest shook with his laughter. His laugh was so light and free, it made my stomach warm to see him like this.

I grinned, chuckling a little. "Okay, it was a little funny, but I hope I never have to see that guy again."

Luka grinned, eyes alight with mischief. "He lives here, and he's one of my best friends. You'll see him all the time." He beamed at me, his white fangs tinged pink with my blood.

I swallowed hard at that statement. All the time. Like … we were just going to go on and do this forever. I wanted to get married and have kids one day, not be tied to this … situation … for eternity. That was depressing, so I just pushed it deep down into my worry-about-this-later portion of my brain.

"Well…" I pulled the edges of my shorts down to cover the bite mark on my inner thigh. "I gotta get going."

Luka's face was a mask of calm now. It was like he let out little bits of joy before realizing what he was doing and then shoved it all back into his grumpy, sexy, silent vampire package.

"Happy Hunting. Isn't that what you all say?" His voice was devoid of emotion, and I shouldn't feel guilty but I did. I was hunting his friends, his family.

"Everyone we hunt has proven crimes against them," I reminded him.

"Right," he grumbled. "What was my crime?"

Oh, he wanted to go there? I hadn't even wanted to think about the reason why I'd been tasked to hunt him that first night at Bang. But if he wanted to go there, then I totally was. "The girl you murdered ten years ago. Took her on a date and bled her *dry*."

He tipped his head back and cackled, a full on sarcastic laugh that gave me chills. "Complete and total fabrication," he deadpanned.

I stilled. "No ... it can't be..." Was he saying Chief Baker was wrong? That Maz was wrong?

Luka pressed me: "Okay, when was it? Where? What was her name? What did she look like? Was there a DNA sample of mine at the scene?"

I stumbled backward, confronted by all of these questions. A dark pit opened inside of me and I feared I would fall in and never make it out.

What was he saying? He never hurt a girl? The story was made up?

Luka shook his head, face softening. "You better go."

I nodded, turning around and headed for the door. When I put my hand on the knob, something came back to me. A memory.

"Luka, why did the Shadow Bloods want you?"

The Shadow Bloods were sent to kill Luka the same night I was. Coincidence?

"I'm not sure you're ready for that answer, Aspen." His voice came from directly behind me and it sent chills up my spine.

I think he was right. I think he could feel the walls I'd built around myself slowly crumbling and he didn't want to shatter them. With a nod, I opened the door and left. Dreading having to come back tomorrow. Dreading facing a truth I suspected would ruin everything I'd built my life upon.

Vasquez, Sterling, Liv, and a dozen of our best hunters all crouched behind the barn, pulling weapons left and right. I had my newly sharpened katana in one hand and a stake in the other. We were all wearing our watches and waiting for the kill order to come in from Maz, who was at society headquarters. Music bled through the thin walls of the barn as the smell of blood filtered through the air.

Feeding party. Vampires' idea of a kegger. We were in Green Bluff, a farming town just outside of Spokane, where you could kill someone and no one would hear their screams.

"I love raids," Julia, a junior hunter with a pretty impressive kill record, whispered as she gripped her stake.

Liv grinned, double fisting her stakes. "I'm feeling quite stabby."

Something felt wrong about this and I couldn't put my finger on why. I loved killing vampires, it was literally all I had wanted to do since I was born … but after Luka told me they'd all started out human … now I just felt muddled about it all.

I mean, if I was attacked and turned into a vampire, would I drink blood to survive? Probably, yeah … as long as it didn't hurt anyone and they were willing. Would that make me a demon? A monster?

Oh, God, help me. I felt sick that I was even questioning my reality like this, everything I thought I knew. I shook my head, trying to clear my thoughts, when our watches buzzed with a text.

Okay, hunters, you are approved to exterminate all vampires and werewolves present. Happy Hunting - Maz.

I frowned.

Wait, werewolves?

Since when did we hunt werewolves? That wasn't in the House of Rose's rulebook. The Thorns,

Ashes, and Skulls sure, but we stuck strictly to bloodsucking vampire demons.

"Yeehaw, let's party," Vasquez called and stood, running around the side of the building. Sterling and the rest followed, but I hesitated, reaching out to grab Liv's arm.

"Werewolves?" I whispered.

Liv shrugged. "Must be some baddies here. Come on."

We'd never been approved to kill the wolves, they weren't in the *Hunter Scriptures*, and it felt wrong. A dark feeling came over me, one that made me rethink everything.

Liv had already run off to the side of the barn, but I stayed where I was.

If God made you, he made me too.

Luka's words pinged around my head until a sob formed in my throat.

No. Stop it. I'd seen a bloodsucker drain young women before. I was seventeen and I'd pulled him away right before he'd raped her. Most vampires *were* bad.

Focus, Aspen. Trust Maz. Trust the society.

I took off in another direction hoping to catch the ones who ran for the fields. I trusted Maz, I trusted God, this was my purpose, what I was made for.

And I'll bet there were over a dozen scared human feeders in there to prove my point. Women usually, being coerced, paid, or compulsed to give their blood to some old creepy-ass vampire. It was wrong.

"I heard Luka is poised to take over the monarchy," a female voice trilled, and I froze.

"Well, he's hiding out pretty good for the month of mourning, that's for sure," a male countered.

Luka take over the monarchy? Month of mourning? Only the hunters thought Luka was dead, clearly these people didn't believe that lie.

"I'm surprised he's still alive with every royal putting out a hit on his head," a third voice joined, and my stomach dropped.

Other royals were putting out hits on Luka? Well, I guess that made sense with what the Shadow Bloods said and his own aunt Morgana ordering the hit on him, but … why? Because he was staging a coup? Was Luka Drake trying to become king of Vampire City?

A scream rose up into the night and I knew it was showtime.

"Hunters!" someone yelled, and then the barn

doors flew open and the party erupted into complete chaos.

I jumped out from where I had been lurking and raised my katana. The three vampires who'd been talking were halfway across the growing cornfield, but two other figures were running right for me.

Wolves.

Their furry paws pounded the ground as they ran. I could see the terrified look in their eyes. We'd just come in and busted up their party and now they were running for their lives. Werewolves … creatures I knew little about because it wasn't my job to hunt them. The other hunter factions took care of stray weres, fey, and even trolls. The witches pretty much kept to themselves and they were the hardest to fight because you couldn't tell a witch from a human unless you caught them doing magic. As I stared at the wolves running at me, teeth bared in fear at my brandished katana, I did a gut check with myself.

Were these two wolves evil? Did they just kill a human? Not that I knew of, so why was I playing God and just expunging them from this earth because they weren't human?

I lowered my sword and backed off to the left, allowing them to pass.

I thought of Sage and Walsh, the kind wolves who'd driven me six hours in a van to hold up my cover story while I was passed out in the back. What if these wolves were them? It was too dark to tell. I wouldn't kill needlessly.

As the wolves darted past me, I stared at their retreating forms with shaking hands. What was I doing? What had I become?

I was so wrapped up in my thoughts, I didn't sense the bloodsucker until it was too late. A male vampire slammed into me, taking me to the ground. I fell backward, hitting the hard-packed dirt as my katana slipped from my hand.

Okay, I wasn't going to needlessly murder were-wolves, but I *would* defend myself against an attack. The vampire straddled me and I pretended to go weak, allowing him to reach up and wrap his hand around my throat. Pulling my arms between us, I came up hard with the tip of the stake, stabbing him right up through the chin. He immediately let go of my throat and fell backward, reaching up to claw at the stake imbedded in his face.

I kicked out, shooting up into a fighting stance and leaning over the male, the dark moonlight casting macabre shadows across his face.

Shit.

He was barely a teenager. Maybe fifteen at the most.

He yanked the stake out of his chin as blood spurted from the wound and I stumbled backward in shock.

What was happening to me?

I … I couldn't kill him. He was a kid.

We were all human once. Some of us didn't ask to be changed.

Luka's voice echoed in my head.

No.

I couldn't do this, not right now. Mental breakdowns were for nights alone in the bathtub, not in the middle of a raid.

The kid stood and came at me, a menacing look on his face as he brandished the stake, swinging at me violently. I dodged to the left, then the right.

"Stop!" I shouted.

Pulling my other stake out, I held it before me so that we were in a dance. Each of us trying to stab the other in the chest like some vampire video game.

"Just go! I'll let you run," I said.

Because I've gone insane and Luka had infected my mind with crazy ideas.

His eyes flared with so much hatred then, I knew I was going to have to kill him to get out of this. He *hated* me and he wouldn't back down, I could see that. I mean, to his credit I had just stabbed him in the face.

I stepped backward five paces. "Just let me go," I told him, trying to find a way we could both survive this. He was a teenager, maybe even forced to be a vampire. I could no longer in good conscience mindlessly kill the bloodsuckers.

He peeled his lips back from his teeth, which were full of blood from my stab wound, and hissed. He lurched forward and I froze, readying myself for the attack.

I can't do it. I can't stab this kid in the heart…

A shadow passed to my left, and then Liv leapt between us, coming across the kid's neck with her sword in one clean arc, removing his head completely.

A strangled cry left my lips as his head hit the ground with a thump.

Liv spun, wide-eyed. "What the hell, Aspen? You froze!"

My hands shook, I couldn't breathe; the world was getting smaller, the weight of it crushing in on me.

"I … I … can't." I dropped my stake and turned, taking off into the night as trees blurred around me.

I crossed the farm at record speed, speeds that I shouldn't be capable of even with my DNA upgrade. I didn't want to know why I was running so fast or what was happening to me. I was vaguely aware of Luka's consciousness right there with me. He felt so close. Liv screamed my name but I barely heard it. I was gone, running into the night with nowhere to go, lost in the darkness of my own moral guilt.

I was a hunter of evil … but how many innocents had I murdered in my blind quest to expunge the demons? Or people who I'd thought were demons?

I ran until my legs felt like they would fall off. My lungs burned as I sucked in gulps of air. Skidding to a stop in the middle of some field, I leaned on my knees and breathed deeply. I was there for ten minutes, trying to calm down my heart and steady my breathing, when I heard the rustle of leaves.

"Are you trying to kill me, woman!?" Liv appeared out of the fields, panting and red faced. Her body was covered in vampire blood. Her sword hung at her side, snug in its scabbard.

"I can't do this anymore, Liv." I raked my hands through my hair. "I think … I think some of the people we're killing are innocent."

Liv looked like I'd shot her. She reeled back, eyes wide. "Innocent! You've heard the reports from

Chief Baker. Rapes, murders, you've seen them drain humans!"

I nodded. "Once. I've killed over seventy vampires and I've seen them kill someone one time."

Liv rolled her eyes. "What are you getting at, Aspen?"

I shrugged. "Have you ever met Chief Baker?"

Liv froze, going very still. "Aspen, you're asking dangerous questions."

"And you're taking blind orders!" I shouted at my bestie, and immediately regretted it when she winced.

"I'm sorry. I'm just … losing it." A sob ripped from my throat. "I'm totally losing my mind."

Liv's face morphed into an angry scowl. "This is what happens when you play with the devil, Aspen. You're feeding a vampire. You're keeping him alive. And it's changing you."

I chewed on my lip. "Did you ever think about how vampires were all human like us once? That some of them might not have wanted to become what they are? That they're just feeding on humans because it's the only way to stay alive?"

Liv's mouth opened in shock. "Aspen! Who are you?"

Her words slashed into the very core of my

being, causing an ache to spread throughout my chest. "I don't know anymore," I told my best friend honestly.

Liv nodded, stepping closer and opening her arms to pull me into a hug. "We'll get through this together. It's a rough patch and we're going to get through it together, okay?"

I squeezed her so tightly then that I knew it must have hurt, but she didn't say anything. I needed her. She was my life raft, the only thing I could trust to keep me afloat right now when I didn't even trust my own thoughts.

The next morning I awoke to find Liv already gone for the day. I decided to go for a workout and forget all the nonsense from last night. Sterling and the others had seen me run off after chickening out about killing the young vampire kid, and we'd had to call for them to pick us up, so there was no getting around what I'd done.

As if thinking about him had summoned my ex, I turned the corner and there he was, leaning against a wall, typing something on his phone. He looked up when he saw me and frowned. "Hey. We need to talk."

I'd been avoiding him, and this talk. I kept using

excuses like I needed to heal after the gala, and I was busy, but it was time to hash it out. Now was a horrible time for me to look deep inside of myself for feelings about Sterling, but I didn't want to lead him on; I wanted to come clean.

I nodded, walking up to him and looking him right in the eye. "Talk."

He cleared his throat. "I want to move back and be with you again. I've missed you." He reached out and touched a lock of my red hair.

So he didn't want to even talk about my running off last night. Good. I needed to rip the Band-Aid off and hit him with a truth bomb.

"Here's the deal, Sterling. You were the first and only man I ever loved." My throat tightened. "But you broke my heart in such an epic way that it's not possible for me to be with you again. That's like self-abuse, and my heart will wonder why we would go back to someone who hurt us like that. I'm just not capable of loving you again after you threw me aside like trash when I bared my deepest feelings to you." Tears streamed down my face as I gave him the raw truth.

His mouth hung open, pain crossing his features. Before I knew what was happening, he pulled me into a hug, wrapping his arms around me so tightly I started to sob. Even though this was the man who hurt me, I'd never felt so safe as I did right now in these arms.

"Fuck, Aspen. I'm so sorry. You're right. You deserve better. I have issues and you deserve better," he rasped against my neck.

Hearing him admit that he had issues and it wasn't all on me was like a weight had lifted off my shoulders. I pulled back, wiping my eyes with a smile.

"So … we're friends from here on out? That feels weird." He ran a hand through his blond locks.

I nodded. "Friends forever. I'll be married and you'll be a forty-year-old hunter dating all the twenty-year-olds like Leonardo DiCaprio, and bringing them to my kids' birthday parties, but we'll always be friends."

He grinned, shaking his head, but there was a sadness in his eyes. "I wish I could be what you want, Aspen. I wish I could jump headfirst into lifelong commitment, but I'm just…"

"Scared? Stupid? An idi—"

He reached out and lightly smacked my arm, causing me to laugh.

"Okay, maybe some of those things," he admitted.

I felt a hundred pounds lighter, and I was actually glad we had this talk.

"I'm always here for you," he told me.

"Same," I said, and gave him one last hug before walking away and leaving behind a huge part of my life. I finally got the closure I needed and it felt damn good. Now I just needed to find Liv and tell her all about it.

As I was heading down the hallway to check the gym room for Liv, I felt Luka's presence overwhelm my mind. *'Can you come get your friend before Izzy kills her?'* he growled.

My eyes widened. *'What? What friend?'*

'The one you came to Bang with. She just broke into my apartment and tried to kill me.'

Liv! That crazy woman. What was she thinking?

'I'll be right there. Don't hurt her!'

I could feel his frustration through our stupid bond. *'I can't make any promises if she wakes up and tries to take my head off again.'*

'Dammit, Luka, she's my sister. Don't. Hurt. Her.'

I tore off down the hallway, then made a left out into the foyer of the society.

He was silent. *'Just hurry. Izzy has a sword to her neck and I can't hold her back forever.'*

Oh God.

I ran past Finn, who started to say something, but I waved him off. "Sorry, hunter emergency!"

"Careful, lass!" he called out.

The second I hit the outside alleyway I took off like my ass was on fire. I needed to save my idiot best friend and not get her killed.

Jumping into my Beetle, I threw it into first gear and took off through the city. By the time I pulled up to Luka's apartment, I'd been honked at three times and flipped off twice. I skidded into a spot and tore out of the car, taking the steps up to his door two at a time. When I burst onto his floor, I found Luka waiting in the doorway. He was shirtless, a thin bead of crusted blood at his neck.

Razor wire.

His tattooed abdomen was covered in small, puckered scars I'd never noticed before—stake marks.

Holy hell, he'd been staked that many times!

How had I not noticed until now? I guess because I kept trying to avoid looking.

"Where is she?!" I yelped.

"I'm fine, thank you for asking," Luka said dryly.

I waved him off and burst into the apartment to find Izzy with the tip of her sword to my bestie's neck. Liv was out cold, lying on the floor with the razor wire in her hand. Luka's blood was all over it.

"You can take that off her neck," I growled to Luka's cousin.

She raised an eyebrow at me. "Oh, is that right?"

"Izz," Luka warned, his presence coming up behind me.

Izzy pulled the blade back and I knelt down before my bestie. If Luka hadn't recognized her as my friend from that night … she'd be dead.

"Thank you." I looked up at him. "She's … important to me." My throat tightened as I hooked an arm under Liv's leg and another under her neck.

"Sisters?" he mused, looking from her brown skin to my pale complexion.

"Yep." Might as well be. Screw genetics. Liv knew me better than I knew myself.

"You're just going to let her go?" Izzy seethed, gripping her sword tightly.

Luka looked amusingly at his cousin. "I don't think it would behoove me to kill my feeder's sister."

Feeder. Ouch. I mean … I was, but he'd never called me that before.

Izzy stepped closer to Luka. "They're insane. They're in a cult. Tell them!" she growled.

Luka's gaze snapped to her. "Stop."

"What?" I asked her. "What did you just say?"

Bitch wasn't going to call me insane and live to tell about it.

Izzy chuckled, shaking her head. "Tell her or I will," she threatened.

I frowned, and opened my mouth to ask Luka what she was talking about, when Liv groaned in my arms, waking up. She was heavier than a sack of rocks but I clutched her tightly to my chest while my back buckled under the strain.

Luka looked at Liv. "Better get her out of here and make sure I never see her here again."

I nodded, pushing everything else aside, and stepped out the front door, starting down the steps.

"Can you come back later for … dinner?" Luka mused, his eyes lighting up when he spoke as if his comment about dinner would be funny.

I groaned. "I'll try to slip out, yeah."

Now wasn't the time for a feeding. I needed to get Liv home and shake the shit out of her for almost getting killed.

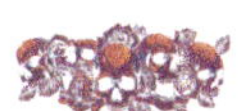

"I'm sorry," Liv groaned, holding an ice bag to her head. "I thought I could fix everything for you by taking him out."

I sighed. "Luka is a Drake. Royalty. You are a junior hunter—"

She peeled her lips back and sneered at me and I held up my hands. "Okay, but, Liv, you could have been killed if he hadn't called me to get you."

Liv frowned. "Why did he do that? I wouldn't have done that to my assassin."

She looked about as puzzled as I felt when it came to all things Luka.

I nodded. "I know. He's different. It's confusing. We're just going to chalk it up to a flaw in the system."

Liv's frown deepened. "I don't like thinking a vampire is a decent person."

I chuckled. "Girl, you have no idea."

"We need chocolate."

"We most definitely do." I walked to the fridge and pulled out the milk and chocolate syrup, then went for the Oreos. When Liv and I said chocolate, we didn't mess around. Chocolate cookies dipped in chocolate milk.

After the fourth cookie, Liv looked sideways at me. "Maybe he's … I dunno."

I laughed. "Don't try to figure it out, it will shatter your world. He's Luka. He's not evil. We just need to leave it at that."

She nodded, taking another cookie, but there was a wild look in her eye, the same look that I probably had when I started to question my own sanity. It felt good to come to terms with the fact that Luka was just one of the good ones and it felt even better that Liv agreed.

I opened my mouth to say something else when Maz texted me.

Maz: Come to my office. I want to talk.

I froze, cookie halfway to my mouth.

Liv peeked over my shoulder and winced. "I'm sure it will be fine."

Yeah right, she'd probably heard about last night and my running off. I was feeling too lost and too confused to really be scared. If she found out what was going on with Luka and I, there was nothing I could do about it.

I KNOCKED on Maz's office door and she called out for me to enter. Opening the door, I found her at her desk, reading the *Hunter Scriptures*. Her giant computer monitor sat to the right, the glow casting a bright light across her face. I had idolized this woman so much, and now I didn't even know if I could trust her.

"You wanted to see me?" I asked, stepping deeper inside the office as Maz set down her book and looked up at me with kind eyes.

"Come sit, dear." She pointed to the chair in front of her desk and I nervously made my way past the large mahogany bookshelves and slipped into the brown leather chair. My gaze fixated on the furnace at the far wall of her office. I wondered how many of those kills were really necessary.

She followed my gaze. "You almost died in Portland. It's normal after that kind of trauma to freeze up the next time you go hunting."

I breathed a little easier. She thought that's why I froze up? I nodded, but decided to dig a little deeper. If Maz was telling the truth with everything, then there was nothing to hide.

"Maz … I just have been thinking a lot lately about who we kill and why—I mean … not vampires in general of course, because I know they can be evil, but more specifically…"

I paused, trying to read her face, which was completely blank and devoid of any emotion.

"Well, there was a fifteen-year-old looking kid vampire at the raid last night and I … just started thinking maybe he didn't want to be changed into a bloodsucker. He was human once, and…"

Understanding dawned in her features and she smiled. "Your moral values were tested because he looked too young? So innocent? Oh, honey, that's a good thing. That's your God-given innocence showing."

I relaxed a little. "Yeah. That's what I thought."

Maz's fingers flew over the keyboard as she looked at the screen before her. I sat there, waiting, unsure what she was doing, until she called me over.

I stepped over and went around her desk. On the screen was the young boy from last night, the one Liv killed.

"Was that him?" Maz asked.

He looked so innocent in this picture, a mop of curly blond hair.

Chase Bolen, it said below the photo.

Then I scrolled through the other information present.

Looks sixteen, actually thirty-seven. Wanted for murder, assault, stalking, breaking and entering.

My eyes bugged at the information.

Maz clicked an arrow and a photo of a dead

woman sprawled out on the carpet of an apartment came into view. A floral couch sat behind her. There was no blood, no big wounds that I could tell; she just looked pale and was unnaturally lying there. My eyes flicked to her neck, where there were two puncture marks.

"Simone Freesome. Human. Twenty years old and on a basketball scholarship at Gonzaga University," Maz told me. "Chase killed her a few months back."

I chewed my lip and she pulled up another photo. "This is Conner. He was at the raid as well. Stephanie, Harper…" She flipped through a bunch of photos all showing their name and age and a list of what they'd done wrong as the walls closed in around me.

I'd been so stupid to question this. To question Maz.

"I … I'm sorry. It's just been a rough few weeks," I told my mentor, my mind spinning.

Maz nodded. "I understand, dear. It's good that you question these things. It means you're human and you have a beautiful heart."

I nodded, forcing myself to say the next few words. "Can you show me what Luka Drake did?"

Maz stilled, her hand frozen over the keyboard. "Your kill from a few weeks ago?"

I dipped my head. "It was … hard. He seemed … normal."

Maz shook her head. "They all do, dear."

Her fingers flew over the keyboard and then she pulled up Luka's photo. My heart twisted into a lead ball in my chest, constricting my breathing.

Luka Drake, looks twenty-two, actually thirty-two. Prince of the Drake royal line. Crimes: Murdering his own father, rape, draining a feeder.

The room spun as I looked at his crimes. Luka killed his father? Rape? Bile rose in my throat as I clasped my hands together to keep them from shaking. "Do you have … evidence?"

Maz gave a curt nod, pulling up a photo.

I took one glance at the redheaded girl sprawled out in the woods with two prick marks on her neck and turned away.

My heart pounded so loudly in my chest, I was sure Maz heard it.

He lied. He was a murderer and rapist and he *lied* to me. I'd been tricked. I'd played with the devil and lost the game.

Concealing any of my emotions from my face, I reached out and clasped Maz's hand.

"I feel better. Thank you," I lied. I felt like I wanted to throw up. I felt like I wanted to take a razor wire to Luka's neck.

Maz nodded. "Of course, dear, you can always come to me with this stuff."

I left her office feeling a heavy depression settle over me. I knew there was only one cure.

Luka Drake had to die. No more games. It just needed to be done.

"THAT LYING BASTARD." Liv was still fuming, even after we'd arrived at our remote cabin in Montana. Yaak, Montana, was literally in the middle of nowhere, surrounded by nothing but trees, wide open land, and moose. Just like I liked it. It lacked people and grocery stores and even cell service, but it was a safe haven for hiding out. Rumor had it that the CIA had cabins along the Yaak River for when they needed to disappear. Liv and I bought a tiny cabin last year in case we ever needed to bug out. We'd paid cash for it and no one from the society knew about it, including Maz.

We'd told Maz we were going on vacation to San Diego and then we decided to hunker down in the cabin on the river while I dried Luka out and he starved to death. From what the book said, it would be a rough few days for me as well, but then it would be done and I wouldn't need to worry about it anymore.

I couldn't kill him outright, he was too human to me, but I could withhold his meals. After seeing the picture of the woman he murdered and knowing he'd lied to me, I just couldn't do this anymore; it was eating at my soul to live this double life.

"This is the right thing," I told Liv as we pulled my Beetle up to the river house.

In the winter, this place was blanketed in snow, but right now, in late summer, it was perfect.

"I missed this place," Liv sighed, as I directed my car into the little overhang carport.

"We should take the canoe out, do some fishing before you really start feeling it," Liv offered.

I nodded, the knot in my stomach tightening with each passing moment. I was going to starve Luka Drake to death.

Every time I felt bad about it, I pulled up the mental image of the redheaded girl he'd killed.

Raped.

Fresh hot anger rushed through me and I nodded, grabbing my duffle bag as Liv and I stepped onto the porch.

I'd turned my phone off so that it couldn't be tracked. Even though there was no cell service here on the Yaak, I wasn't taking any chances.

The sun was going to set in a few hours, so Liv and I made quick work of readying the house for our stay. I turned on the well pump, dusted off the furniture, and opened the windows while Liv started up the refrigerator and transferred the contents of our cooler into it.

After that, we pulled the old canoe out and brushed off the spider webs.

"We haven't been up here in ages. Feels good to get away." Liv smiled as she looked out at the river and our sad little dock that was in desperate need of repair. One post had sunken in, making it crooked, and I felt bad for not taking better care of this place. Montana was God's country; everywhere I looked I saw his perfect design. Liv and I had gotten this place for a hundred grand. It had a composting toilet, well, and solar electricity. The perfect off-grid house.

I sighed, letting the nature and fresh air settle into my bones and give me strength for the task ahead.

The sun was still out, warming us with its rays as we launched the canoe out onto the water. We paddled as we passed other houses, waving at some of the older neighbors who didn't know who we were.

I'd convinced Liv to buy this place after my twentieth kill. Hunters had a shelf life of about twenty-five to thirty years. Finn was pushing it. In fact, now that I thought about it, he was the oldest hunter in our Spokane branch, save for Maz. All that violence and danger eventually wore you down or took you out. It was actually Sterling who told me it was a well-known thing that hunters had little bolt-holes they stashed away for the day they would retire … if they weren't killed in action. By then your face was well known in the supernatural community and so you just faded away into some small town where no one knew your past.

This place would do until Liv and I could upgrade to our private island.

"Do you think he can sense where you are?" Liv asked suddenly.

My eyes widened. "Luka?" I could feel him just under my skin, like a thought waiting to pop into my head. "No. No way." I wasn't actually sure, but that idea horrified me.

Liv relaxed a little, slowing her paddling as the

water's stream carried our canoe. "And it will take three days to kill him?"

I mean, I didn't exactly know, but hadn't he said he needed to feed every two days to survive?

"I think so," I added.

Liv looked happier at that, nodding curtly. "In four days, this will be a distant memory, and we can go back to hunting and never speak of this again."

That was one thing we both agreed on. "Ever. Ever. Again," I agreed.

We fished for an hour, catching two large trout before heading back to hunker in the cabin. Looking over at my bestie, I thanked God for her. I wouldn't be able to go through this with anyone else.

That night, we ate a good dinner of grilled lemon-seasoned trout and potatoes. After playing two hours of Scrabble, we said goodnight and I tucked into bed in my little room at the far end of our small cabin.

As my eyes were drifting off to sleep, I felt him.

'Aspen? I thought you were coming over? Everything okay?'

I swallowed hard, guilt worming its way into my chest, but again I pulled up the image of the redheaded girl and pushed the guilt down.

Rape.

Murder.

Lies.

Ignoring Luka, I fell asleep.

The next day was rough. I felt as sick as a dog from the thirst symptoms Luka must be having. Headache, chapped lips, dry mouth no matter how much water I drank, and uncontrollable anger.

'Aspen, are you hurt?' Luka checked in with me for the fifth time that day, and I was having a hard time ignoring him. *'Where are you?'* Maybe it was the thirst, maybe it was the anger about the way he lied, but my resolve was thinning.

"Don't talk to him," Liv snapped at me as she brought me more ice chips from the freezer.

"I'm not!" I growled.

"He is a rapist and a murderer. A demon like all the rest," Liv told me, and I nodded.

"I know," I whimpered, a single tear falling down my cheek.

Did I know? I'd seen the photo, but why was my gut telling me something else?

If God made you, he made me too.

I shook my head, trying to dislodge the thoughts from my brain.

No.

Over the next five hours, Liv blasted music, fed

me soup, played cards and even charades, all while I was curled into a ball on the couch, ignoring Luka's pleas and dying from the worst headache I'd ever had in my life.

'*Aspen!*' Luka's voice was so desperate I couldn't take it anymore. '*Tell me where you are and I'll save you. I'll come for you.*'

He'll save me?

'*I don't need to be saved. I need you dead,*' I seethed with hatred, finally addressing him. '*You lying, murdering rapist!*' I hurled at him as the rage of the thirst finally consumed what pleasantries were left in my body.

I felt Luka recoil as if I'd stung him.

'*They got you. They fully got you,*' was all he said, and then he went silent.

They fully got you? What the hell was that supposed to mean?

My mind chewed on that for hours.

They fully got you.

If God made you, he made me too.

I'll come for you.

My thoughts were a delirious jumble.

Finally, at midnight on the second day, when Liv was brushing a cool cloth across my forehead, I broke into sobs.

"Make it stop, Livvie. Please."

I looked up at my best friend to see tears line her eyes. "I wish I could."

Sobs wracked my body as I felt Luka's presence slip away and our bond grew fuzzy as blackness took me. Was it only day two? Or was it already day three? Time was so weird. I'd changed clothes and I was no longer on the couch.

"Liv?"

"You passed out." She looked at me with wide eyes; dark circles hung like bags under her black lashes.

I felt for him, for Luka, and burst into tears when I came up with nothing. Just an open void where he once used to be.

I didn't realize how much of myself had been enmeshed with him until now. Until he was gone.

"He's go—" Before I could get the words out, the door burst off its hinges and splintered in half.

Liv wasted no time throwing herself forward into an army roll and grabbing her katana.

In the doorway stood three women I recognized.

Sage, Demi, and Isabella.

"You little bitch!" Isabella seethed.

They were here for revenge. They were here to kill me, and I was so weak and frail right now there wasn't a damn thing I could do about it. Izzy rushed forward, but Demi reached out and yanked her by the back of the neck.

"I got this. Stand *down*," the alpha growled.

Izzy froze, lowering her head in submission.

Whoa.

I'd never seen anyone subdue a vampire like that.

Sage was looking at me with pity as she and Demi strode across the room and over to Liv, who was ready to fight them both to protect me.

"Stand down," Demi growled, her eyes flashing yellow, and Liv went stock still.

I gasped as I realized what was happening.

Demi had the gift of compulsion.

A wolf? How? It wasn't supposed to work on us … my mind reeled as I prepared myself for the inevitable.

Demi strode past Liv, her long blond hair swishing at her back, and my eyes fell to her t-shirt.

It's a good day to leave me alone, it said with an image of a sloth hanging in a tree.

Any other day and I would have liked this girl; we would probably be friends. But she was an alpha werewolf who had just compulsed my best friend and was now here to revenge-kill me. She was my enemy.

I grabbed the remote, clutching it loosely in my hand as my body started to shake from thirst symptoms.

Demi looked down at me and shook her head in disappointment.

"Listen, Aspen, I hate to be the one to tell you this, but you're in a cult. They lie to you, make up profiles on the vamps you kill to assuage your guilt, and trick you into murdering them. Luka's a good guy, an innocent guy, and you're *killing* him."

Cult? Fake profiles? Did she think I was stupid? Maybe it was the three-day headache or the lack of sleep, but I found what she'd just said hilarious. Tipping my head back, I laughed, deep and throaty.

Demi crouched onto the couch and leaned inches from my face. I swear I saw the ghost of a wolf flash over her face then. A white one, but then it was gone.

"Listen, *hunter,* you think you know about the supernatural world because you've killed a few vampires? Seen a werewolf? You know *nothing*. You have no idea what we deal with, blind to your human eyes."

Chills rose up on my arms.

"What do you mean?" A lump formed in my throat as the hilarity of it all wore off.

"I don't have time to enlighten you right now. I need you to save Luka," she barked.

"I'd rather die than save that demon!" I snarled.

She bared her teeth. "That is a problem for me because he's my husband's best friend and the future king of the vampires. If we can win him the crown, we can be sure to end the war with the vampires. So, I need you to get up and feed him and knock this shit off!" With that, she gestured to the open doorway and I peered out to see the same helicopter from before.

Was Luka in there right now?

"No!" I shouted in her face with as much anger as I could muster in my delirium.

Demi cried out in frustration, raising her arms up into the air. "I'd force you to do it, but Luka said he'll only feed from you willingly."

I didn't believe her. He was dying, of course he'd feed from me right now whether I wanted him to or not!

Demi snapped her fingers, and Izzy rushed forward and handed her a smart phone. The female alpha looked at Liv, who was flattened against the wall, staring at us both. "You might as well both see this," Demi told her, and then called Liv over.

"Show them how you do it—quickly," Demi instructed Izzy.

Izzy nodded, throwing a glare my way, and sat on the edge of the couch as Liv and I looked expectantly over at her phone.

"What is th—?" I stopped as I saw her tap an app called VHS. When it opened, "Vampire Hunter Society" scrolled across the screen and then four logos. I gasped when I saw they were the four hunter Houses of Rose, Thorn, Ashes, and Skulls. She touched the House of Rose logo. The app opened and my jaw unhinged when Izzy tapped the word "Mark."

She typed in Luka Drake and then uploaded a photo of her cousin. Liv and I stared wide-eyed as she then used a dropdown menu to select her bounty price.

It wasn't until she tapped "Choose Your Hunter" that a whimper left my throat.

There, next to Vasquez and Liv, was my picture. It had my stats underneath: kill rating, age, everything. All of our names were there. "I'd have taken you deeper into the app but this is all I can access without WiFi." Izzy looked sideways at me as she closed the app and canceled the hit. "There are no families or chief of police that hire you. *We* do. Rival vampires, fey, witches, whoever. You're hired assassins," Izzy said blankly.

"No," Liv whimpered, shaking her head vigorously.

I'd noticed that the lowest bounty able to be paid was twenty thousand. But we only got five. That meant Maz was taking seventy-five percent. Bile rose in my throat as my body went into shock. Nothing was real.

"Aspen, it's not real. This is a trick," Liv said.

But I knew in my bones that it wasn't and I didn't feel anything about it. I just felt numb, cold, void of … anything. My tower of beliefs had just been knocked down and I was crushed between the rubble.

My whole life was a lie.

I stood, unsteady on my feet as I began to shuffle towards the sound of whirring helicopter blades outside. I started to fall forward when I got to the doorway as dizziness overtook me, but Sage caught me.

"Don't do it! It's a lie!" I heard Liv wail, but the tone of her voice was full of heartbreak. She felt the truth as I did.

With Sage's help, I walked barefoot and shivering across the yard toward the open helicopter door.

Sawyer, the other alpha, was at Luka's feet, his head hung low in his hands. My eyes flicked to Luka, who was barely conscious. His body was shriveled inward, like a rotting cucumber, and it killed me to know that I did that to him. Sawyer's head snapped up as I stepped onto the helicopter and Sage helped me to kneel at Luka's side.

"Let's give them privacy." Sage yanked on Sawyer, who didn't move, he just glared down at me with fearsome glowing yellow eyes.

"You better save him or I'll kill everyone you care about." The alpha's threat sounded real, but his voice was laced with hurt.

Sage pulled him backward and then it was just me and Luka. Tears rolled down my face and dropped onto his bare chest. He was so pale, so near death, and it was all because of me. His eyes tracked me, but he didn't move.

A sob ripped from my throat. "Why didn't you tell me? If you knew this whole time, why not tell me!"

Luka reached up with a shaky hand and caught a chunk of my red hair in his brittle fingers.

"I … thought your faith … was kind of beautiful. I didn't want to be … the one to make you…" His voice was so soft and weak, I had to lean in closer to hear him. "To make you hate God."

My throat constricted as I tried to swallow the tears, but I couldn't; they flowed freely down my cheeks.

Did I hate God?

No. Never. God didn't lie to me and distort things so that I believed the fabrication. If anything, God was my only source of comfort right now, my guiding light in this darkness.

It was Maz who I now reserved my hatred for.

My entire world had shattered, and she had to be in on it.

I nodded, unable to stop the flow of tears.

This man had saved my life more times than I could remember, and all I'd done was call him horrible things and try to kill him.

The app Izzy showed me could be fake, but I doubted it. Either way, I'd decided to save him. The empty feeling in my chest where he used to be was too lonely. I wanted him back.

"Drink," I commanded, holding my wrist to his dry, cracked mouth.

His eyes flared orange, almost turning red. "Why?"

I looked down at him, searching myself for that

answer. "Because right now I can't imagine living without you."

He was a blur of movement as he ignored my wrist and reached up to grab the back of my neck. Pulling me down to him, I felt the pressure of his lips on my neck, and then the addicting sharp pinch of his teeth sliding into my vein. Pleasure rushed through my system as I bit down on my moan. With each slurp, each beat of my heart, my headache eased, my thirst faded, and my bond to Luka opened up like a dam bursting.

Luka's presence filled me up, enmeshing with the very core of me. It was like I'd gained a window into his soul. I felt him in a way I'd never felt anyone before. There was so much light in him, so much love and kindness, but also … a hidden darkness—a scared little boy who had been through unspeakable things. I gasped as his fingers wound into my hair, pulling me closer to him.

'I see you, Aspen Rose.' His voice was like a balm to a wound that had been festering inside of me for weeks. I felt him probing at the edges of my mind, my soul, my heart. It was hard to explain, but whatever this was … it was magic. Whether it was good or bad, I didn't know, but I did know that it had tied

me to Luka forever in a way that I wasn't sure I really would ever understand.

Feeling the blood pour out of me, easing all of my symptoms, Luka started to slow his gulping. This was by far the longest feeding we'd ever had, and I started to feel dizzy. Just then, he pulled away from my neck but didn't release his hold on the back of my head. I pulled back a few inches until I was face to face with him. My red blood coated his lips, and his honey colored eyes regarded me in a way that I couldn't explain. He had never looked healthier and more alive; there was a pink to his cheeks, and his chest was plump with rock hard muscle, dewy with a light dusting of sweat. He'd gone from near death to looking like he'd just come out of the gym.

"Aspen?" he whispered and my brain went fuzzy.

"Yes?" I panted, unable to make myself pull away from his light touch. He reached up and traced my cheek with his fingers.

"I think we need to kiss now and get it out of our system," he stated flatly.

My eyes widened. Kiss him? That was so far against the rules that—

The rules were a lie though, weren't they?

"I'm sure it will be awful and then I can stop

fantasizing about it," he added, which caused a half-cocked grin to pull at the edges of my mouth.

"I'm awful at many things. Scrabble, drawing, eating with chopsticks. But kissing isn't one of them," I said, and his eyes went half-lidded.

He was waiting, waiting for me.

Maybe he was right; there was obvious sexual tension between us, and one kiss could just smash it and get it out of the way.

I licked my lips, wetting them, and decided to just go for it before I could think on it any further. Leaning forward, I brought my lips closer to his.

"Oh good, you're not dead," Sawyer's voice called from behind me, and I snapped my head back, my cheeks reddening.

Luka groaned, and I cleared my throat.

"Oh shit, sorry." Sawyer seemed to have understood he interrupted something, which was beyond mortifying.

"I better check on Liv." I stood as Luka sat up next to me. I stepped closer to the male alpha and pinned him with a glare. "Does this mean you won't be killing everyone I care about?"

He grinned. "I've torn up my hit list."

My brow furrowed, because I couldn't tell if he was kidding or not.

"You threatened to kill her family? Geez, man," Luka said from behind me.

"She tried to starve you!" Sawyer shot back. My gaze flicked to a tattoo at his collarbone, one I recognized.

Five Crew.

My head swiveled back to a shirtless Luka, and there on his collarbone was the same thing.

Interesting. They had a little gang and it was kind of adorable. Walsh and Bennet had the same tattoo…

I stepped across the lawn and into the house, when I heard Liv wail. "Just go! You lying witches! Get out."

Oh no.

"Livvie." I strode inside and Liv broke away from where she was on the couch and threw herself at me. "They're lying, the app was a lie. It has to be!" She broke into sobs and I met Sage's, Demi's, and Izzy's gazes just behind her.

"I think you guys should go now," I told them.

The truth was, I thought the app was real, but I needed more proof than that. Maz was … family … and I couldn't believe she would knowingly lie to us like this. Maybe she was tricked too, and I had to find out who was doing this to us and put a stop to it.

The three girls nodded and moved to leave.

Izzy stopped, looking over at me curiously, her black glossy hair in stark contrast to her glowy white skin.

"Shall we bring Luka back tomorrow for his feeding or…?" She was making sure I wasn't going to pull this stunt again.

"I'll be back in Spokane tomorrow. I'll come to him," I told her.

She nodded curtly. "In case you were wondering how we found you, we had a witch track you. We can find you anywhere you try to hide."

Great. Point taken.

They left then, the fading whirr of helicopter blades marking their absence.

Liv pulled back from me and wiped her eyes. "What if its real? What if we are hired assassins? Just killing bloodsuckers for other bloodsuckers?"

I swallowed hard. "Then we'll find out who's tricked all of us and take their head."

Liv nodded in grim determination at that.

As we quickly packed our things and closed up the house, readying it for another stretch of long months unused, I started to think of hundreds of small little things. Connecting the dots.

Like the way that all of the House of Rose

hunters were orphans. The way that Maz hadn't really seemed to age the whole nineteen years I'd known her. The fact that there were no hunters at the House of Rose over the age of twenty-five—I'd assumed they all retired or died like Sterling said, but ... what if they found out? What if they were silenced?

An epic knot formed in my stomach as Liv and I started the three-hour drive back to Spokane.

I couldn't stop asking myself the same question over and over.

What if *I* was the bad guy this entire time?

L iv and I agreed to say nothing to Sterling or Vasquez or any of the other hunters until we had more information. We arrived early the next morning back at the society and I started to make a plan.

"If you can make sure Maz is out of her office, I can sneak in and try to find something on her computer," I told Liv, who was basically catatonic on the couch with red-rimmed eyes. She couldn't believe our entire life might be a lie. I'd accepted it, and moved right on to the anger phase of grieving. I wanted proof, and then I wanted to hurt whoever was doing this. She was still in denial.

"Maz gets info on the marks with photos of victims. I can check her emails and see who sends them to her. Maybe the chief of police is the ring-leader." I really didn't want Maz to be the bad one.

Liv just nodded absently. "What if her computer is password protected?"

Shit. "Then I'll guess a bunch of passwords. It's probably something from the scriptures."

Liv rolled her eyes. "You need a hacker, Aspen. One with blond hair, blue eyes, and is about six-four tall."

Oh crap. She was right. Sterling was really good with computers, but our new friendship was fragile, and I didn't want to ask for a favor so soon after rejecting him.

"Take one for the team, Aspen," Liv said flatly.

"Fine. I'll get Sterling to help, but no one else. We can't trust anyone right now."

Swallowing my pride, I went in search of my ex-boyfriend.

I found him in the gym lifting weights with Vasquez. He was shirtless, glistening with sweat, looking like a freaking bathing suit model.

When he saw me, he perked up. "Aspen."

I ran a nervous hand through my hair. "Hey, can

you meet me at my apartment in ten? I need to talk to you."

He nodded. "Oh sure. I'll shower and be right over."

I bobbed my head and then left, hoping Sterling would take the news well.

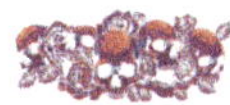

"Are you insane!?" Sterling whisper-screamed as Liv and I sat around our dining table.

I'd just told him I needed to break into Maz's office.

"No, and I wouldn't ask you if it wasn't of the upmost importance," I told him.

He scowled at me. "No, not unless you tell me why."

Bastard. Liv and I shared a look, Liv shaking her head no. "I think someone has been lying to us and I need proof," I said vaguely.

Sterling wasn't buying it. "Lying about what? Proof about what?"

I growled. "Sterling, it's me! Don't you still trust me?"

He barked out a laugh. "Don't use our past relationship, which you are so clearly over, to talk about trust. I saw you get carried out by that vampire at the gala. I saw you order those wolves to save me, so tell me what's going on or I'll go to Maz."

Shit. This had taken a turn for the worse.

There was no way I could tell him I'd bonded with a freaking vampire, but maybe I could make up a story that wasn't too far from the truth.

"I went out to kill a mark at Bang and instead he saved my life."

Sterling's face screwed up in confusion. "Why would he do that?"

I waved him off. "It doesn't matter. Through him, I… befriended those two werewolves who saved you, and one of them…" I figured Izzy didn't need to be in this equation. "Showed me an app where vampires and other supernaturals, order hunters from any of the Houses to kill their bloodsucker enemies."

Liv nodded. "I saw it. It's like Uber Eats but you order a vampire head instead."

Sterling's mouth popped open and then he tipped his head back and howled in laughter. "Ridiculous," he said.

I shook my shoulders. "Help me prove that. Maz has files on her computer from Chief Baker. We need to find out if the chief is even real."

Sterling's eyes bugged at that. "Why wouldn't he be real? This is crazy."

I stood, slamming my fist onto the table. "Then prove me wrong, Ster! Show me I'm crazy and this is all fake."

He crossed his arms in defiance. "Fine. But I don't need to go into Maz's office to do that. I can do it from here."

I went stock still. "Say what?"

Sterling let out a deep breath. "The entire House of Rose is on a linked network. I helped Maz update it two years ago. Get your laptop."

Holy freaking crap, I scrambled out of the room so fast I nearly tripped.

Grabbing my laptop off my bed, I bolted back to where Sterling and Liv were waiting for me. Handing Sterling the laptop, he popped it open and I used my thumbprint to unlock it.

"Watch this." His fingers flew over the keyboard and there was a network of names that he was scrolling through. Zia's computer, Vaz the Stag, Livvie, the entire hunter network was here.

I pointed a finger at him. "You don't spy on my computer, do you?"

He shook his head. "I have better things to do,

but Maz had me build this backdoor in case she ever needed it for security reasons."

I raised an eyebrow and Liv looked at me suspiciously. "Security reasons?"

Sterling clicked on one called *The Eagle* and nodded. That must be the name of Maz's computer. "Sometimes hunters leave the society, or they get married to humans, or they go with another house like the Thorns or the Ashes. In that case, she can wipe their mainframe from her desk the second she gets wind of them leaving so they don't take trade secrets."

I swallowed hard. I mean … I guess that seemed normal. We were a secret society after all. But it also meant Maz could spy on us and control information we received. The knot in my stomach grew as he pulled up a desktop identical to the one Maz had open the other day.

"There." I pointed to the "Marks" folder.

Sterling opened it and there were hundreds—no thousands—of names of vampires we'd killed.

"What am I looking for?" he asked.

"I dunno, just start opening stuff," I told him.

He opened one, Greggory Shores, and pulled up the bio.

Looks twenty-five, actually fifty-seven, wanted for murder, rape, and draining a feeder.

"Click on the evidence," I urged him. There was a picture attached.

Liv went stock still and I reached out and grasped her hand. Sterling double-clicked the photo, and when it popped up both of them gasped.

"Sick bastard," Sterling growled.

"He deserved to die," Liv agreed.

I was frozen, mouth open in shock. It was the same picture of the redheaded girl Maz had shown me that proved Luka was guilty of rape and murder.

"Go to Luka Drake." My voice cracked with emotion as the walls started to close in on me.

Liv must have noticed the change in my voice, because she looked up at me as my eyes filled with tears.

Sterling opened Luka's file.

"Evidence photo," I croaked.

He pulled it up and we all stared at the same redheaded girl, the same pose, the same wooded background.

"Wait, what?" Liv said.

"It's a mistake," Sterling said coolly, but I heard the unnerved tone in his voice.

"Open more," Liv growled. "Open them all."

We watched on in horrified silence as Sterling clicked through each and every picture. They all used one of three photos. The redhead, the brunette female, and the blond male. All of them.

All. Of. Them.

Someone had played us. They'd probably called each one of us into the office and showed us one or two pictures to instill our loyalty.

"I can't breathe," Liv said, as fresh tears rolled down her cheeks.

"Hang on, this… is a mistake," Sterling offered.

"You didn't see the app! They ordered us like a fucking cheeseburger!" I cried out, pacing the room.

Maz knew… she had to know.

"The other houses?" I stopped dead. "Are they all in on it?"

Sterling looked like he might be sick. "I don't know."

"We're Shadow Bloods. We're hired assassins with no morals who do it for the money." My voice was devoid of all emotion.

Liv sobbed, and I wanted to comfort my friend, but I was having my own mental breakdown at the moment.

"Money," Sterling said, and then his hands went wild at the keyboard. He smashed away at the keys, pulling up window after window while I tried to keep up. He muttered a few curse words under his breath, but was going through things too fast for me to keep up.

"What is it?" I asked.

Sterling looked up at me like a little lost puppy. "Maz... she has millions. *Millions.* And all of the senders had offshore accounts. Not... local grieving families."

No.

Liv's crying just... stopped, and I could see the moment she went numb.

She peered up at me, and it reminded me of the look on her face when she was fifteen and made her first kill. She'd looked so lost and confused; the first kill was always the hardest.

"Aspen, I want to leave, right now. I can't... I can't stay here." Her voice was so robotic, I knew she was at the end of her rope, her sanity cracking.

"Okay. Let's pack a bag. We'll stay at a hotel and figure this out," I told her.

Sterling put his hands out. "A hotel? If this is true... if... Maz won't let you just leave with this knowledge. You need a credit card to book a hotel, and then she'll find you."

Liv slammed her fist on the table, causing both

Sterling and I to jump. "I'm not staying here a second longer!"

"I know where we can go. Maz won't find us." My eyes flicked to Liv's, and she raised one eyebrow.

I had to go and feed the bastard every day anyway. Might as well hole up with Luka while we figured this out.

"Come with us," I told Sterling. "We need to see how deep this goes. Does every house know? Every country? I need to know everything."

Sterling sighed, leaning back in his chair. "If you want to know how deep this goes, you'll need someone on the inside. I'll bring Vasquez in on it, and we'll stay and get more information. Build a case to show the others."

Emotion clogged my throat. Sterling was a good guy. He may have been a shitty boyfriend but he was a decent human. I rushed forward and pulled him into a hug.

"What will Maz think when we're gone?" I asked him.

He shrugged. "I dunno… I'll tell her you ran off to be with a vampire."

I froze, chills running up my arms as I looked for any indication that he was kidding. He wasn't.

"Ster… it's not like that."

He waved me off. "Just go. Get a burner phone, call me every day, and we'll meet at Riverfront Park to exchange any information I find in two days' time."

Liv stepped forward and we pulled her into a group hug, holding each other tightly. The entire world that we belonged to had just cracked at its foundation, but we still had each other.

When we pulled back, I glanced at Sterling's face to see the shock starting to settle into him as well.

"There are some really bad vampires in this world. I've seen them destroy people, suck them dry. We... we are still doing good by taking them out," Sterling said almost to himself.

Liv and I exchanged a look. He didn't see the app, didn't see how other vampires chose us to kill their enemies.

"There are bad humans in this world too, Sterling." I gave him a side hug. "I'll see you in two days. We will lay low until then."

Liv and I shoved everything we could into our hunting duffle bags, but left our smartphones and laptops on the table. Sterling wiped them of all information with a few keystrokes and then left to go back to the gym. With our katanas on our backs and the keys to my Volkswagen Beetle in hand, Liv and I walked the halls of the House of Rose for the last time.

If anyone saw us, it would look like we were going hunting. I just prayed we didn't run into Maz on our way out, because if we did I was going to rip her head off.

We passed Kenz and my heart pinched. Was he in on it? He was old, he'd been here forever. He was dusting the entryway table as we passed and looked up, giving us a warm smile.

"Happy Hunting," he said, and my stomach filled with bile.

That sentence no longer carried any weight.

We were murderers; we'd become the very things we despised. With a curt nod, I didn't trust myself to speak, we exited the entryway doors, waved to Finn, and then left the society the same way we entered it —two orphans lost and alone in this world.

I knocked on Luka's door, clutching my duffle bag as Liv stood next to me, tears silently sliding down her face. When he pulled it open, he took one look at the both of us and ushered us inside.

"I… we…" My voice cracked. "…need a place to stay for a bit."

He nodded. "You can stay as long as you like. Bennet and Izzy can bunk together and you can have Izzy's room," Luka said.

"The hell they can," Izzy growled from behind me.

Luka shot his cousin a glare and she grumbled.

"Fine. For a few days. Then they need to figure something else out."

I nodded. Everything felt so… dark and heavy. The realization that we'd been lied to our entire life pressed in on me until I felt like I couldn't breathe. Luka crossed the hall and opened the door to Izzy's room. Isabelle slipped inside and grabbed a few things. "New sheets are in the hall closet," she said with what little excitement was possible as she left the room.

Liv tore the old sheets from the bed as I stared awkwardly at Luka, who stood in the doorway.

"I… need to talk to you about something, but it can wait." He rubbed the back of his neck and I nodded as Liv slipped between us and came back with a stack of clean sheets from the hall closet.

"Thanks for letting us stay. It's just until we can figure out…"

Our lives? Our jobs? Our entire reality? Did we seriously just leave the society? My chest felt tight suddenly as I forced myself to try to take deep breaths. I was on the verge of a panic attack.

Was I living with a vampire now? How the hell had this happened?

Luka swallowed hard. *Are you okay?* His mental voice caressed my thoughts and I settled a little.

'No, everything I was taught was a lie,' I answered truthfully.

Luka frowned, nodding. "Goodnight, Aspen."

"Good morning actually," I said, knowing this was his awake time. Sunset was when vampires had the most energy.

He grinned, and holy hell my knees nearly gave way. I wished he wasn't so good looking, I wished right then that I'd been bound to a big ugly fat vampire. One I hadn't almost kissed.

He stepped away and I closed the door, turning around to find Liv curled up into a ball in the corner of the bed. The second I flipped off the lights, she broke into sobs and my heart shattered into a hundred pieces. Kicking off my shoes, I padded across the room and slipped into bed with her, wrapping my arms around her.

"We're going to get through this." I wished my voice was as strong as my reassurances, but it betrayed me.

Liv whimpered, grasping on to my arms. "Will God forgive us?"

I thought about her question long and hard. We'd done all of this in God's name, only to find out it was really in Maz's name…

But if there was one thing I knew about God, it was that He was forgiving.

"Yes. We just have to navigate things from here on out the right way. We can't go back to senseless killing. There are plenty of humans that need to be protected from bad vampires. We will focus on those and no longer blindly take orders."

She nodded, her tears drying up as some of the heaviness left my chest.

Yes. That's what we would do.

An idea formed in my mind then. A wild idea, a huge idea.

What if Liv, Sterling, Vasquez, and I started our own hunter house? One that only killed in self-defense, and one that protected. A bodyguard service for humans and supernaturals. Because Luka was right. God made everything under the sun, and that meant supes too. If they had souls, which I believed they did, then I would protect them with my sword.

My mind spun for an hour thinking of all the details, calculating the money that it would take and how much I had, plus what Liv had in savings. We could totally make it happen. I was thinking of hunter house names as I finally fell asleep, feeling at peace with my place in the world and my moral duty to right my wrongs.

THE NEXT MORNING I awoke with a headache and remembered that I should have let Luka feed last night, but of course in my disturbed state I'd forgotten and he was kind enough not to ask. I shook Livvie awake. Her eyes were puffy, and she looked like she could use hours more sleep.

"No," she groaned, and rolled back over.

I grinned. "I want to open our own hunter house. One that only kills in self-defense and protects humans and supernaturals alike. With Sterling and Vaz too."

She shot up from her pillow so fast she almost cracked into my forehead. "You want to play body-guard to supes?"

I shrugged. "Only the good ones. Like Luka, Sage, the other werewolves I met who saved my life. They were good people."

I saw the moment the idea clicked with Liv. She grinned. "This would make amends for all the … bad … we'd been doing." She winced, unable to say *mindless murdering rampaging*.

I nodded. "What do you say?"

She grinned. "Only if Vasquez is the janitor. Then you have a deal."

I tipped my head back and laughed, finally feeling good about this situation. We were going to turn some lemons into lemonade!

She rolled over to go back to sleep and I slipped out of the room and brushed my teeth, tying my hair into a topknot and changing into jean shorts and a tank top. Some deodorant and dry shampoo and I was ready to be fed on by a stupidly hot vampire who I now apparently believed had a soul…

I was pretty sure I'd lost my mind and was now living in some delusion. Stepping out into the hallway, I padded across the kitchen and then went up to Luka's door, poising my hand over it to knock.

That's when I thought of our almost kiss in the helicopter. I was going to know this guy for the rest of my life. Kissing was a horrible idea. Right?

"Come in. I hear your heartbeat," Luka said, and I groaned.

Stupid human heartbeat.

Pulling the door open, I saw him sitting up in bed reading with his side lamp on. He had a green apple sucker, the ones they dip in caramel. "Good morning, Aspen." His voice was husky; I hated when he was so formal.

I curtsied. "Prince Luka," I said in a mock English accent.

He grinned, pulling the sucker slowly from his mouth, and my gaze fell to his chest and the tattoo that peeked out of his powder blue cotton tee.

"What's Five Crew?" I asked, shutting the door and crossing the room to sit at the foot of his bed. He watched me walk over, eyes running shamelessly down my bare legs as my cheeks heated.

Reaching up, he touched the tattoo at his collarbone. "Sawyer, Walsh, Bennett, myself, and someone you haven't met yet, Talon."

"You all have the tattoo? Were you like a little gang?" I laughed.

He didn't return my cheeriness. "Something like that."

My stomach dropped, and I was reminded of his time in prison. "From … your time in Magic City Prison?"

He seemed to consider. "Aspen, just ask me what you really want to ask me," he said flatly.

I swallowed hard, running my fingers along his clean cotton sheets. "What did you do to get in there?"

He looked me right in the eyes, vulnerability passing over his features. "Are you going to believe me?"

A pang of guilt sliced into my chest and I nodded. "Of course."

Two days ago, I was trying to kill him. I didn't blame him for not trusting me with his secrets.

"I did nothing to be put in prison. I pissed off my aunt, the queen at the time, and she threw me in there because the law states she couldn't kill me without losing her leadership position."

My mouth popped open. He did nothing? That was anticlimactic.

"What did you do to piss her off?" I mean, from what I'd heard it wasn't that hard to accomplish. The queen was a complete psycho.

His eyes darkened. "I was born."

Okay, this was clearly a touchy subject. "I'm sorry, I—"

He held up a hand. "No. It's fine. It's just a deep wound."

I swallowed hard and nodded. "I came to..." I waved my wrist in front of him, and he gave me a halfcocked grin.

Luka was a blur of movement. One second he was on the bed and the next he was kneeling on the floor before me, taking my wrist gingerly into his hands.

Holy hell on wheels. My belly warmed.

"Aspen?" He looked up at me seductively and my throat went dry.

"Hmm?"

His gaze fell to my bare legs and my giant rose tattoo, and then slowly trailed their way back up my body. "If you want me to behave, then please stop wearing those tiny shorts around me."

My mouth popped open in surprise, and then he pressed his lips to my wrist. His teeth slid into my vein and ecstasy exploded inside of me. My heart pumped frantically in my chest as pleasure coursed through my entire body. It hit me then … it didn't always feel euphoric like this, especially not when I was mad at him for two weeks after the gala. My feeding pleasure was linked to my feelings for him at the time—that blew my mind.

Because I was feeding him daily now, the feedings were shorter. He pulled away from my wrist quickly and licked the last drop of blood, all while holding my gaze.

Lord help me.

"Maybe I don't want you to behave." The words had barely left my lips before he sprang from his knees and placed a hand behind my back, pushing me gently onto the bed and lowering himself over me.

Breath hitched in my throat, and I swear my heart leapt into my stomach. I couldn't take my eyes off of his red-tinged lips. What would it be like to kiss him? Cold? Stiff? Salty?

"Say it," he growled, in the most dominating, sexiest voice I could imagine.

"Kiss me," I commanded, knowing that's what he wanted to hear, finally realizing that I didn't care anymore that he was a vampire. I just didn't care. I could feel his soul, sense his goodness.

A halfcocked grin pulled at the edge of his mouth, then he lowered his lips to mine. I inhaled in anticipation, and the scent of the caramel apple pop hit my nose a second before his mouth pressed to mine. A slight moan escaped me as Luka tenderly pressed his lips to mine. It was a soft kiss at first. Eager but innocent. Then I parted my lips and the innocence evaporated like rain after a storm. Hungry pleasure burst between us as our tongues crashed together in a kiss that said so much more than words ever could. I could taste the sweetness of the apple sucker mixed with a salty brine that I realized was my own blood.

This kiss was otherworldly. I'd never been kissed like this in my entire life, not even by Sterling, and he was the best kisser I'd ever had. When you were a virgin, you got pretty good at making out. Kissing was my jam, I had perfected it, I was a connoisseur of kisses. Slow, sweet, fast, hot, I liked them all, but this…

This kiss broke me and put me back together in the same moment.

This kiss was epic.

I'm kissing a vampire, I thought wildly as he pulled my bottom lip into his mouth and sucked it.

A sudden knock at the door had us both going still. With a groan, Luka pushed himself off of me and looked down at me with a satisfied gaze as I scrambled to sit up, wipe my lips, and smooth my hair.

Holy crap, I just kissed Luka Drake!

He opened the door and Isabelle was standing before us, glossy black hair braided over one shoulder. There was a folded letter in her hands with a red wax seal to clasp it. It was like one of those old-time letters you would see in a movie.

"It's arrived." Her voice held fear and trembling, and I sat up straighter.

Luka took the letter from his cousin, peered over

his shoulder casually at me, and then tore it open. His face scanned the page and I tried to interpret his features in order to glean any information from him.

"I've been chosen," Luka said, his voice devoid of any emotion.

Izzy nodded, looking partly relieved and partly horrified. After a moment of them standing there staring at each other awkwardly, she rushed forward and pulled him into a hug.

I lowered my gaze, feeling weird for intruding on their obviously serious moment. When she pulled back, she looked at me. "Is she on board? You'll need a constant feeder if you have any hope to survive."

Survive? Constant feeder?

Luka looked over at me. "I haven't asked her yet. I've been meaning to."

"Ask me what?" I stood.

Izzy gave him a nod and then left the room and closed the door. Luka pinched the bridge of his nose as if he had a headache.

"Remember how I said I needed to talk to you about something last night? I've been summoned to Vampire City by the elders to compete for my rightful place as king."

"Oh. I mean, that's what you wanted, right?" Demi had said that she needed him to become king to stop the werewolves and vampires from going to war again.

He nodded, then thought better of it and shook his head. "I mean yes, I want things to change, but I don't relish the idea of spending the rest of my life tied up in meetings and bureaucracy."

"You said compete," I reminded him, wondering what kind of competition this would be.

He dipped his chin. "I knew this letter would be coming, I wanted to talk to you about this sooner, but you had your own problems to worry about."

Yeah, like my entire life being a lie.

"What's the competition, Luka? Why would you need a constant feeder?" I stepped closer and his body reacted, tightening and coiling as if luring me in.

"The ten strongest heirs have been chosen to battle to the death for the crown. If I'm the last one standing, I get it."

I involuntarily leaned my ear forward as if I didn't hear him right. "Luka … a battle to the death with nine other vampires?"

A slow and devastatingly sexy grin pulled at his lips. "Yes. It's a good thing I'm a wicked fighter who just spent a lot of time in prison literally kicking asses every day."

I rolled my eyes. "Well, if you could win by the size of your ego, I think they would crown you right now."

He chuckled. "So you'll help me? I mean normally … I'd have a handful of feeders there, but since I can only feed from you…" He chewed his lip nervously and I swallowed.

"This will be in Vampire City? For how long?" Because I had plans to start my own hunter society…

He nodded. "The whole process can take up to a month."

"A month!" I shouted.

He winced. "But after that, when I'm king, you can … go back to your life here if you want, and I can come to you daily. It's only an hour drive."

The future king of the vampires was going to drive into the human world every day to feed from me?

That meant…

"So if you're king, you'll live there? In Vampire City? Forever?"

He inclined his head, vulnerability crossing his features. "I mean, you could live there too if you wanted … but I figured with your distaste for my kind—"

"Yeah, I probably wouldn't be able to sleep at night," I told him honestly.

He chuckled. "Fair enough. Just for the month, then? Liv can come too. You will have my full protection and be there as guests of a prince. Nothing bad will happen to you."

Now it was my turn to chuckle. "We're vampire killers. I'm not worried about it."

He inclined his head. "Is that a yes? I can't tell."

I opened my mouth to speak when my burner phone went off in my pocket.

The only person who had this number was Sterling.

I opened the archaic flip phone and hit the green button. "Hey."

"Let's meet at the place. Now."

My eyes bugged. "Right now?"

"NOW," Sterling pressed; there was a wild tone to his voice. Something had him unhinged.

Crap.

"I'm on my way!" I snapped the phone shut and looked to Luka, who had concern etched all over his features.

"I … gotta go, I'll be back in an hour." I tore out of the room and into the hallway.

"Need help?" Luka was a blur behind me.

"I'm good," I told him as I grabbed my purse and slipped a stake inside from my hunting bag, which sat by the door.

"If Liv wakes up, tell her I went to meet Sterling and I'll be right back."

Luka's eyes went stormy. "Sterling the ex?"

I nodded. I'd be lying if I said I didn't enjoy the look of jealousy that passed across his face.

With my mind fully on Sterling and what he might have uncovered to pull me to our meet-up spot a day early, I fled Luka's apartment and that amazing, steamy kiss.

15

I threw my Beetle into park and jumped out onto the sidewalk at Riverfront Park. It was bustling with activity on this hot summer day with a ton of families out and about. The snow cone food truck had a line of twenty people. I tried to peer past them and onto the bridge where Sterling would know to meet me. After we talked about whatever it was he wanted to tell me, I was totally inviting him to start the new hunter firm with Livvie and I. It felt so right and I was so excited about the prospect of being able to be in control of who I hunted and why.

I peered around, past the laughing families and people on bikes but saw no sign of Sterling. Where was he? I glanced at my burner phone when something caught my eye on the bench near the duck pond.

It was a small cardboard box, and on this side facing me was the House of Rose logo…

He must have left the package and bolted. Maybe he was worried about being followed. Crossing the space quickly, I slowed as I reached the box; the lid was popped slightly open. When my gaze fell on the crimson fluid dripping out of the bottom right corner of the box, my stomach dropped.

No.

It was like time stopped. I reached for the open box flaps, pulling them apart, and my gaze fell on the head of the only man I'd ever loved. A bloodcurdling scream ripped from my throat and it felt like my soul left my body.

Sterling.

Dead. Beheaded in the way that we beheaded the vampires. Who would…?

Maz? Did Maz catch him sneaking around and … no, she wouldn't, right? A thousand thoughts smashed around my brain and I must have blacked out, because before I knew it, I was back at the snow cone truck, no memory of even running there. My hands shook as sobs wracked my chest and I looked around the park, lost in my thoughts. The vision of Sterling's dead face was burned into my mind, torturing me.

A kind older woman with a red snow cone approached me. "Miss, are you okay?"

I was bawling, legit ugly crying in public, and I couldn't stop it. I didn't want to stop it.

Sterling.

The memory of the night I first told him I loved him washed over me. I could smell him in that moment, taste him, feel him. And then the guilt that I'd dragged him into this whole thing bubbled up inside of me. He was dead because of *me*.

I was halfway down the street to my car, sucking in huge lungfuls of air as cars and bike riders and passersby stared at me like I was a lunatic. I stopped and leaned against the wall of a building, trying to catch my breath.

Then the sobbing stopped as if it never started and then full blown rage consumed me.

How. Fucking. Dare. She.

How dare Maz kill Sterling just for finding out her stupid secret. She wanted to preach about evil and sin and then she went and fell in love with money! The greatest evil of all! She used all of us in the name of God to squirrel away millions. I would expose her if it was the last thing I did. And after that, I'd take *her* head.

It had to be Maz, it had to be.

Using the back of my hand, I wiped my tears and shook myself.

I needed to tell Liv and we needed a plan. Because if Maz took out Sterling … we were next. I prayed Vasquez hadn't been pulled into this, because even though he was a cheating douchebag, I didn't want him dead.

God, please help me and protect me. I sent up a silent prayer to the big man upstairs. I might be currently confused about the details on how God worked, but I knew God was real and it wasn't his fault Maz perverted his word and brainwashed us to kill in His name.

With renewed strength, I pushed off the building and beelined it to my car. I slowed my pace when my gaze fell on the scrawny bike messenger. He looked my age, leaning up against his bike and tapping his phone. There was a manila envelope in his hands. He looked up at me expectantly.

"Aspen? This your car? The guy said you would have bright red hair and drive a yellow Beetle." The dude stepped forward and I flinched, ready to take his damn head if he tried anything.

He extended the manila envelope to me and I took it.

"Later." He looked at my no-doubt puffy red eyes and backed up, getting back onto his bike and riding away.

I stared at the top of the envelope and my hands shook as I saw my name scrawled in Sterling's neat handwriting.

Looking over my shoulder to make sure I wasn't being watched, I slipped inside my Beetle and took off. I wasn't sticking around here for a second longer than I needed to. The image of Sterling's head in the box was still flashing in my mind no matter how much I tried to dislodge it. Weaving in and out of traffic, I pulled into the first church parking lot I could find and threw the car in park.

I didn't know what was in this folder, but I wanted to be alone when I read it. If it was from Sterling, then I *really* wanted to be alone.

Reaching into the envelope, I pulled out a stack of papers, focusing on the handwritten note on top first.

ASPEN,

If you are reading this, it means I'm dead and Vasquez

activated my fallback plan of sending this to you via courier. He will have gone into hiding, don't worry about him.

I paused, my eyes becoming too blurry with tears to read any further. A silent sob wracked my chest as I wiped my eyes on my t-shirt and kept reading.

After you and Liv left, I stayed up all night and kept digging. I found out the most disturbing information you could ever imagine. Aspen ... I was never a great boyfriend, but I want you to know that I did love you and this information will shake you. Please prepare yourself.

I put the note down, my heart hammering in my chest as fear rose up inside of me. Why would he say that? How bad could it be? I mean, what was worse than finding out your religious leader was a fake and embezzling money? It was not lost on me that the first time Sterling said he loved me was just right now in this letter. Maybe it was something he could only bring himself to do if he thought he was going to die. As sad as that was, it still brought me comfort. I let out a shaky breath, praying for strength as I read the rest of the letter.

After reading this information, please burn it. Then move to another country and forget you ever saw it. This evidence can never be brought to light or it will seal the death of thousands of hunters all over the world.

Move to another country? Seal the deaths of thousands of hunters? What the heck was he talking about?

I ... I love you, Aspen. Please just be happy. Do whatever it takes to be that.

Sterling

P.S. Maz froze both of your bank accounts and drained them. You're on your own.

I burst into sobs, clutching the papers to my chest. Maz froze Liv and my accounts ... that meant no startup money for our new hunter service. I was genuinely scared to keep reading, but I knew that I must or Sterling will have died in vain.

Pulling the papers back, I set the handwritten note aside and stared at the top page.

My eyes skimmed over everything so fast I wasn't really sure what I was reading. It had my name and my birth weight as a baby.

Aspen Rose

Born July 16th, 2002

7 pounds 6 ounces

I stopped at another name. Something Maz told me they had no information about.

Breeder: Marilee Rose.

I frowned at the word *breeder*. My mother? Was

that … my mother? Why would she be called a breeder…?

When I got to the next line, my entire body stiffened.

Genetics: 86% human, 14% Fey

The air froze in my lungs as I stared at Sterling's cursive note. *Not human?* he'd scrawled.

I shook my head, as if it would wake me from this dream.

Not human? *I* was not human?

I went to the next page and saw…

Olivia Rose

Born October 1ˢᵗ, 2002

Birth Weight: 6 pounds 5 ounces

Breeder: Genevieve Rose

Genetics: 88% human, 12% Fey

Liv. No … this wasn't … this couldn't mean.

I flipped to the next page and bile rose in my throat as I scanned it. The DNA modification shots we received when we were little … those were a lie too, just saline. They were to cover up our fey powers that made us just fast enough and just strong enough to hunt the vampires, but human enough to pass as one out in the real world.

When I reached the final page, I didn't think it could get any worse … but it did.

Aspen Rose, healthy female hunter baby.
$10,000

It was a transaction receipt, signed by Maz herself.

I was bought. Like property, like cattle, like a slave. Maz Rose bought me and Liv and all of the supposed orphans in her care and then brought us up to be assassins. *Killers.*

A scream ripped from my throat as the anger bled out of me. I'd never been this mad, this hurt, this shocked in my entire life. Maz Rose, my mother, my grandmother, my mentor, my everything. She bought me, conditioned me to think I was fighting evil in God's name, and lied to me. My chest tightened as I struggled to suck in enough air. I couldn't breathe. I rolled down my car window, sticking my head out of it as dizziness washed over me. I just wanted to breathe.

Sterling. Dead.

Maz. Lied.

Me. Not human.

Slave.

Fey.

My mind spun and I felt like I was going to pass out. I had no more purpose. I had no money. I wasn't even a damn human. The depression of all of these thoughts weighed down on me until it felt like I was buried alive. Nothing felt real anymore, nothing but Liv and Luka. Those were the only two people in my life who hadn't lied to me.

'*Getting weird vibes from you. You okay?*' Luka's voice bombarded my mind and I swallowed hard.

'*Yeah. Be back soon.*' This crap show was something you told someone in person. I couldn't deal with Luka right now.

I wiped my cheeks, rolling my window back up with shaky hands.

My gaze flicked across the street to my bank. I had to know if what Sterling said was true. Had Maz taken all my money? If she took mine, had she taken Liv's too? How? How could she do that? I never put her on my account.

My hands shook as I opened my car door, leaving it in the church parking lot as I jogged across the road, dodging honking cars. I clutched my ID and bank card tightly as my heart hammered in my chest. All the hunters used this credit union. Maz said we had a guy on the inside and they gave us perks like zero monthly account fees and free retirement account set up and management. Now I was wondering if this guy on the inside watched our money and reported to her.

I had about seventy-eight thousand dollars in my checking account last time I looked, and double that in savings. Not to mention the ROTH IRA I'd opened. I had averaged twenty grand a month in hunter bounties over the past five years and had my eye on an eventual early retirement. If it was gone … if there was nothing left…

"Hello, how can I help you?" the nice-looking blond woman asked from behind the counter. I never came in here, I did all my banking online, but without a smart phone I was going to have to go old school.

I handed her my card and ID. "Can you tell me my account balance please? For both checking and savings." My voice cracked. I was so clearly on the edge of a nervous breakdown.

She gave me a long look, probably taking in my red-rimmed eyes and messy hair.

Taking my card and ID, she nodded, starting to type away at her computer.

"Pin please." She indicated a keypad that sat on the counter. I put in my four digit pin and then held my breath.

Her eyebrows knitted together. "Miss Rose, you closed your accounts yesterday." She frowned. "Your balances are zero."

No.

A sob ripped from my throat and the woman stepped backward a pace. "Are you … okay?"

"Where did the money go? Did I come in and take it out in cash? Did I transfer it? Where is it!?" I growled, slamming my fist on the counter.

The woman's blue eyes widened to saucers and she looked over her shoulder to a male teller. "It was wired, transferred to your other bank account, I presume?" She ended the sentence on a question, like *Why does this chick not know where her money is?*

I didn't need to ask about the IRA. It was gone too, and so would all of Liv's money. My entire life savings … gone. Maybe that was for the best. Maybe I didn't want this lying blood money anyway.

"Can I … help you with anything else?" She pushed my cards back to me.

"No." I grabbed them and turned, storming out of the bank, feeling completely and utterly hopeless. Now I was jobless, homeless, and broke. I had nothing, no purpose. Except … Luka. Luka needed me. He needed to become king, and he needed me to help him do that. Liv and I needed a place to hide out while I figured out my next move. Maybe going with him into Magic City wouldn't be that bad after all. At least Luka never lied to me. Suddenly that kiss with him felt like the only real thing in my entire life.

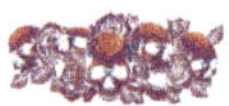

I DROVE like a bat out of hell back to Luka's apartment, and parked my car two blocks away. I jogged the rest of the way, peering over my shoulder the entire time to make sure I wasn't being followed.

I took the steps up to his floor three at a time. All the while I had the papers from Sterling clutched in my hand and I couldn't stop the looping thought in my head:

I'm not human. I'm not human. I'm not human.

I would tell Liv what Sterling had unveiled and we would go hide out with Luka in Vampire City for a month while I helped him become king. Then Liv and I would come back to Spokane and bring Maz and the entire House of Rose down in flames. *Yes,* this idea was the only thing keeping me from going insane right now.

I bolted up the last few steps and yanked the door open to Luka's apartment. I felt so raw right now, so fragile and misunderstood. It was actually a comfort when my gaze fell on Luka, standing in the kitchen staring down at a piece of paper.

Upon seeing Luka, I sighed in relief and he looked up at me.

"Liv and I will go with you," I told him and he smiled, "and you have to see this." I stepped closer to him, holding up the papers in my hand. He was my person now, one of the only people I could trust, which was crazy considering I had tried to kill him last week. But I knew once I told him about the part fey thing, he would help me figure it out and not judge me for not being a hundred percent human.

He didn't take the papers I tried to hand him. He just looked uncomfortably at me, his smile faltering, face pinched in anxiety.

"What's wrong?" I asked.

He coughed into his hand, glancing over my shoulder. "Uh—"

"Hi, sugar plum," a female purred, adding as much venom to the words *sugar plum* as possible.

I spun, looking into the eyes of a strikingly beautiful blond female vampire. She had that alabaster skin and unbreathing thing going on, not to mention the red tinge to her lips. She wore a midnight-blue evening gown like she was going to a ball or something, her hair pulled into a slick bun at the nape of her neck.

I swallowed hard. "Umm, hi? Who are you?"

Now that I felt it, I realized Luka was bleeding anxiety through our bond. I'd been too busy losing my mind to sense it coming off of him.

A feral grin graced her lips and she extended her hand, fingers downward, as if she meant for me to kiss the top. "I'm Cassara Blane, Luka's betrothed."

My brain short-circuited in that moment.

Betrothed?

Wasn't that an old fancy word for engaged?

I reached out and shook her hand lightly, in shock, and then spun to Luka.

'You kissed me knowing you were engaged!' I roared so loud in his head that he flinched.

'It was arranged at birth and I had no say. I thought ... she was dead.' He blanched, looking horrified.

No say? Bullshit.

This day absolutely could not get any worse.

'Then tell her to leave now,' I prodded him, hoping he sensed the wild tangle of emotions within me that were close to completely spinning out.

He winced. *'I can't. I need her.'*

And that was the moment my heart broke into a thousand pieces. Had I really deluded myself into thinking a vampire could fall for me? The emotion clogging my throat and the tears welling in my eyes told me that yes, yes I had.

"Well, the car is waiting to take us to Vampire City, Lukie. Your … feeder … can follow behind us," Cassara said with disdain as she looked at me like I was a cockroach.

Feeder.

Luka paled, as if that were possible, and turned to face me.

'Aspen … I … need you. Please. Are you still with me?' His tone was one of complete and total pleading, his face too. He basically turned into a twelve-week-old puppy, and even popped out his bottom lip at me.

I was in too vulnerable of a place to resist him. I had no one, nowhere to go, and no money. Liv and I needed a place to lie low while I figured out this whole not-entirely-human thing. But after that kiss … after that kiss with Luka … everything had felt different between us, and now to find out he was engaged! It ripped my chest wide open.

'Fine, I'm with you,' I growled, hoping the mental connection was sending him all the angry vibes, because there was a lot of anger here. *'For now,'* I added.

How dare he kiss me? How dare he start something he couldn't finish?

Cassara stepped over to Luka and rubbed a hand along his chest, raking her fingernails down his abs.

"Luka, my love, I haven't seen you in years. I'm anxious to get going," she purred, her cleavage popping out of her dark blue dress.

He swallowed hard, nodding once as I closed my eyes and prayed for strength. If this was God's idea of testing me…

Spoiler alert: I was going to fail.

Preorder book two here!

JOIN THE WOLF PACK

Facebook.com/groups/leiastonewolfpack

ACKNOWLEDGMENTS

Thank you Julie Hall for choosing Aspen's name on a writers' retreat and being a generally amazing human being with beautiful hardback book pretties. Thank you Jaymin Eve for listening to all my rants on how I wasn't going to make this book deadline. I made the deadline! (Barcly). Big round of thanks to my editor, proofer, ARC team, PA's, Wolf Pack, cover designer, and the entire crew that is involved in releasing one of my books. I literally couldn't do this without you! And finally thank you to my family, who always share me with my books because my characters don't seem to shut up.